Centuries Ago and Very Fast

Centuries Ago and Very Fast

by

Rebecca Ore

Seattle

Aqueduct Press, PO Box 95787
Seattle, WA 98145-2787
www.aqueductpress.com

ISBN: 978-1-933500-25-6

Parts of "Centuries Ago and Very Fast" were published in *Dragonfire* (an online publication of Drexel University, inactive).
An earlier version of "Acid and Stoned Reindeer" was published in *Clarkesworld* (online publication) and reprinted in *Wilde Stories: 2008*.

Cover Design by Lynne Jenson Lampe
Back Cover:
Lower photo ©iStockphoto.com/Peeter Viisimaa
Upper photo ©iStockphoto.com/Ben Taylor

Front Cover:
Stone steps ©iStockphoto.com/Warwick Lister-Kaye
Oil lamp ©iStockphoto.com/Monica Lewandowska
White beads ©iStockphoto.com/Stephen Chan
Photo of Mammoth skeleton by Kathryn Wilham

Book Design by Kathryn Wilham

Printed in the USA by Thomson-Shore Inc.

To Adam Thornton, Randy McDonald, Eva Thury, Stacy Ake, and to my agent, Jill Grinberg, who said the longer version just wasn't working, and to the people at Harper Collins who allowed me to not have this count as an option book. Also thanks to Henry Israeli and Nick Mamatus for publishing parts of this in *Dragonfire* and *Clarkesworld*. And to Carol Deppe for insisting that I was a better writer than I thought I was.

Contents

The Sister Who Started It All
[Thomas's Story, Vel's Tale]

When I first met him running on the moors, I thought he was gypsy or part Paki with his otter body and the broad head that ended in an almost pointed chin, but he said he was European, old stock, some French in the bloodlines. His left little finger ended just below where the nail would have been.

We'd been lovers for almost a year—at my flat, in the moors when he could tease me into open-air sex, in cars, but never at his house before he decided to trust me and brought me to the kitchen of his old farmhouse where his kinswoman Carolyn, a doctor, was waiting for us. I wondered if what had been making my cop brain itch would be a crime I'd be obliged to turn him in for. What he turned out to be was *Le Bel Homo*, but not *sans merci*. Vel said, "Here's one secret." He disappeared and flickered back with two fistfuls of coarse chestnut fur, as long as horse mane hair, but different, with clumps of finer hair mixed in. "The other is that I killed that mammoth's calf when I was a boy. I've lived for a long time, maybe 15,000 years. I don't remember it all."

Full of the warm ancient fur, Vel's hands trembled as he extended them to me.

After I touched the coarse long hairs and the soft undercoat, the longevity seemed completely believable. Carolyn, who had kept his secrets as hundreds or thousands of kin before her had, watched us both. She hated having to trust me.

I'd never seen him scared before. I was touched. I said, "We could enter a civil union; then I couldn't be forced to say anything about you."

Carolyn said, "We'll sell the mammoth fur on eBay. People pay $15 for about five strands." She put down the stone knife she'd been holding. I realized that if I'd said the wrong thing, she'd have killed me. *Love you, too, Carolyn.* That's what Vel had been afraid of.

What would I turn him in for, being born 14,000 or 15,000 years ago in a land that had been covered by water?

I walked up the stairs that night with Vel and took a shower in his ensuite bathroom with the most modernistic fucking plumbing I'd ever seen. I think he invented some of it — Paleolithic boy gone silicone happy with hot and cold running water. He had plumbed in a line for enemas. Beside the tub was a basket of hose tips all wrapped in plastic. Vel must have always been an optimist.

I turned on the spigot for the enema hose. "I've never seen one of these before."

"You can adjust the tap for warmer or colder water, but it's not going to get too hot because that's dangerous. I found it online and installed it myself."

I looked around the room. The toilet was behind a door and from what I could see of it, had a basket of goodies within arm's reach — lubes and goops and body oils. "Why not in the toilet?"

"What?"

"That enema thing? Wouldn't it be better to have it as part of the toilet and not part of the bath?"

Vel said, "Sure, but I think I'd need a sink and pipes in the toilet first, and drilling through three foot stone walls is hard."

"That's okay. I've never seen most of what you have here. I've always just used whatever the shop that sold the condoms had for lubricant." Was I to be murdered in my sleep now that Vel had told me his secret?

Vel handed me a huge towel and warmed robe. He was still wearing his little time travel rig of loincloth and leggings, but took them off and went into shower after I did. I sat down on the bed not feeling terribly sexual.

I could smell the soap on his body. If he did live on without aging, there'd come a time when he'd have to leave me.

Curled around my dick, I sat at the edge of the bed while he dried himself off. He put on a robe and asked, "Do you really want to stay the night?"

"I have to work in the morning."

"I'll get you up in time."

"I'm not particularly sleepy, though."

Vel gripped my shoulder, a bit rough, not sexual in intent. I didn't want to look him in the eyes. He said, "I raised one of my sisters who turned into the mother of all my sisters. Carolyn is one of my nieces. Let me tell you the story."

I sat on the edge of the bed while he leaned back against the headboard, wrapped in his robe, eyes dark under brows that were not contemporary.

The Sister of Us All — Vel's Tale

When a woman bore a baby before an earlier baby could walk she decided which baby to keep and which baby to strangle. My mother was with my father still, who hadn't been run off yet by one of the younger men, and I was not quite a man yet, but had learned something about how people who were attracted to their own sex could give pleasure to each other from one of the boys who'd been to the painting caves. He'd lived there for a number of years before we brought him back filled with more languages, a better way to make stone lamps, and knowledge of the prostate and cock root.

The boy looked healthy and vigorous, a shame to put him down. I loved my sister and didn't really want another boy in the family, but Ma had lost two boys earlier, so I knew they weren't going to kill this boy. We all looked at each other, and then I said, "I'll take care of her."

"She's yours. Take her away for the summer so she knows to turn to you for her needs and doesn't try to fight my son," my mother said. "You can get some other kids, your friend perhaps, to go hunting. She's old enough to suck chewed food out of your mouth."

So, a gang of us, people who were my friends until they died, went off with me carrying a baby on my hip.

Ro, who became my lover later, also was carrying a child, but a younger one. His mother had died in childbirth. Ro found someone who'd lost a baby to suckle his brother and had been bringing the wet nurse what meat he could kill or steal until the child could eat chewed meat. The others who went with us were young couples who wanted to practice tending children.

Ma was right. I could kill a male colt and chew it up, and my sister's little baby tongue would winkle it out of my mouth. We spared the one insane male colt who insisted on following us around, the mares, and the male colts who were too little. We also managed to get a mammoth calf separated from its mother and took it down. We built a small-scale hide frame for the girls who found flint and split it for hide-dressing tools and dressed out and brain-tanned the small mammoth hide without splitting it. And we tossed the babies on the hide, and the lighter older girls.

My sister and I spent the summer together. When we rejoined the adults in the fall, we all chased reindeer and went down to the coast for fish, before we made winter camp where the mammoths could be trapped in low country, which is under the North Sea now. My sister learned how to say no. I learned how to chew hides and punch holes for bone needles to pull sinew through, and made her clothes. She remembered her mother, but came to me when she was frightened. Ma still made my clothes, but the new baby took most of her time. We went through a mammoth about every two weeks, along with smaller game. Winter solstice came, and the boys learned how to make fire from the men, and we made fire and passed the lamps around, then took a flame from the fire-plow fire and sent fire following the wicks in these lamps with hollow bowls and handles like bird beaks. And dawn of solstice, we all went out and cheered that the sun had decided to show up and would be showing up more and more until summer solstice with the sun in the sky as long as he'd ever be, and then to the cold and dark again.

And at four, my sister was walking and helping the women with gathering fibers, mammoth in shedding time, plant fibers the rest of the time, and was running errands, fetching small things, so the adult women wanted me to carry another baby, which I did, of course, but my sister had been the first child I raised, and we stayed together until I was raising first her children and then her grandchildren.

I was a minor god. I stayed with the family for three thousand years with it being one year after another. I can't remember much other than we killed off the mammoths. Then things changed. More later.

♋

Vel didn't know what time to wake me for work, so he woke me up around 5:30. I could have slept a bit later than that, but pulled on the clothes I had. He offered a loincloth instead of yesterday's briefs, but I had a spare pair of briefs and my shaving bag in my car. He went downstairs for them while I brushed and flossed and looked over the collection of electronic and Stone Age and Medieval jetsam that Vel had collected. The rooms looked like a geek's room, but now I knew they were the rooms of a Paleolithic boy who'd been following the cutting edges of whatever technology for 14,000 years. The collection of everything from old Sparc Stations to stone lamps to a 1954 Rolleiflex twin lens reflex camera in mint condition to a 23-inch liquid crystal display made sense, given who he was. I was fingering a stone knife when he came back with my briefs and razor.

"You could shave with those. Well, not with that one, but many men in those days used flint razors to go clean-shaven."

I went into the bathroom and lathered up over the sink and shaved with modern steel. He was stubbling up himself, but looked rather tired on top of that. I asked, "You going to shave, too?"

"Um. Carolyn has breakfast for us. Carolyn can be ever so thoughtful when she's really thinking. She asked if I explained any of the consequences of a very good immune system."

I looked at his eyes in the mirror and kept shaving.

He said, "I can get allergic reactions. I can spread things if anything got lodged under my foreskin."

"Things?"

"Semen. Parasites. I don't think I've ever spread AIDS. I mostly avoid..."

"Okay, we'll wear condoms," I said. "Or do you want to promise to be monogamous?"

"And it never happened with the purely oral things, or with hands."

"And your sister wanted you to tell me this?"

"Remember, she's my doctor."

I wondered what 14,000 years of semen up the bum could do, and asked, "Ever have bad allergic reactions?"

"I remember one once, but I'd been with the guy a really long time."

"Did you sleep any last night?"

"No. I was sitting there, remembering. I'll go back to sleep after you've gone to work."

"At least you need to sleep." He could be hurt, had lost the tip of a finger. Someone could kill him — nobody lived long without a head, nor could he survive a burning.

He pulled on sweat pants and a shirt to go down to breakfast with me. We didn't say much to each other on the stairs, and I said my good mornings to his sister who had cooked up sausages, eggs, and toast, and made coffee. Vel smelled it and poured himself a cup and sat down, sipping it.

Carolyn said, "I don't think he should have told you, but you'd figure something out if you lived with him for more than a few years. He thinks he needs you."

I didn't say anything to her, just poured myself a cup of coffee, drank it down fairly hot, and poured another one, needing the caffeine to get moving. Carolyn put a plate by me. I looked at my watch and figured I had enough time for breakfast if nobody chatted at me. Carolyn appeared to have washed the mammoth fur, which was now drying on newspapers. She wasn't kidding about selling it on eBay.

Carolyn appeared to look through me, into the future. She focused on me again and smiled.

Vel wasn't paying attention to anything other than the morning television news about Russia invading Georgia playing on his laptop. Carolyn touched his shoulder, but he just shrugged slightly.

Carolyn said, "I was checking the records after you went to bed. Aren't your people the Trents who married one of our girls?"

Family. I was distant kin. One of ours had taken a wife from them in something like 1840. I was something like five generations from that. My granny's grandmother's mom came from an old family over in Somerset that kept yellow curs and native ponies on land mentioned in the

Domesday Book. And she'd go back to visit her people a few days before Christmas every other year or so, but we'd stopped going by 1902.

Being with Vel felt like coming home. He'd selectively bred his people to be loyal to him, and he needed them to stay sane.

As I was leaving for work, Vel gave me a big old cock-tingling kiss, tongued me almost to gagging. "I thought you smelled right," he said.

I was lucky that most of Somerset behaved fairly well that day as I did the office work, testified in court, drove the roads, and had my lunch at the usual place with the usual mates talking about the stupid urban people wanting to make foxes sacred beings and keep the hounds from going after the stags as has been custom here since the early days.

The red deer had lived here since Vel was a baby in moss clouts. The hounds that chased them then were nearer to wolves than what the hunts used these days. I wanted to go home and recite W.H. Auden to Vel, his head on my arm, not a half, not one-hundredth as ephemeral as me.

Oh, I had this side that I find embarrassing, see, and Vel was bringing it out. I thought I was too old for all this, but Vel was so very much older. England, that has such beautiful men in it, wasn't even an island when Vel was born, and Vel was born in drowned country between here and there.

When the day was over, I called Vel on his mobile to meet me for dinner away from all the weight of the house. We met in an Indian curry place and grinned at each other over vindaloo and walked in the electrically lit streets, looking in shop windows. I loved the play of metal vapor light against brows and jaw that were ancient when the world was lit by whale oil.

"Yer mate's worth looking at," one of the boys standing around waiting for pizza takeaway said.

We all smiled around, and I took Vel back to my place this time. He called Carolyn to tell her not to expect him home that night. No stories for her. No stories for me, either. No words at all.

The end of the beginning.

Queen of the Vid

First person I brought back from a bar on my first visit to New York was a wild Hispanic drag queen, a skinny thing in sateen with heels that looked like she stole them from Tina Turner and a wig that looked half defiant and half insane, all blonde, fiber-optic cables. She worked during the day as a cook at a restaurant that catered to poor tourists just getting off the bus at Port Authority. At night, she spent half her time studying English and the other half going out to the Stonewall. She'd been in a movie, was going to be in a movie, I'm not sure which now, but the movie was *Paris is Burning*. She didn't like white boys, but I was looking darker than usual and I, in New York on business, spoke Spanish.

I don't much fancy drag queens. They shave, for one thing, and lately they've been taking hormones for tits. But I'd heard that they do good cock play, yours and theirs. The wig was pathetic, though. I'd have to buy her a new one I could stand to look at if I saw her more than once.

We went back to the room I was renting in the Chelsea Hotel. I figured she'd steal my money if I fell asleep on her. I'd have to go home for more, but that would give me an excuse never to see her again.

She told me she still lived with her parents on East 117th Street, in a rent-controlled apartment, but they were going to move out to New Jersey sometime and leave the apartment to her. I nodded, didn't tell her that I had family in England or that I'd been around since the Ice.

We'd discussed the price in the bar. I'm not used to paying, but I decided to humor her, just as I suspected her parents were humoring her about giving her the rent-controlled apartment when they moved to New Jersey. So I put $20 on the dresser but stood between her and the dresser. Perform, bitch. I'd have to teach her about bumping dick heads if she didn't know that much, about the thigh-fucking the 20th Century seemed to have forgotten. I wanted her naked and looking like a shaved boy, but that wasn't what drag queens did. She sat down on the bed while I stood and knew how to gently take my balls in her mouth and just how much pressure to put on them. She also knew how to handle a cock that wasn't cut. Most of the white boys in America then were circumcised.

This was getting friendly. I came; she swallowed. Was this $20 worth or could we go for more? I started working up her tight little skirt, then pulled down the panty-hose and felt, *yay*, cock. I'd never heard of real women pretending to be drag queens to seduce gay guys except for that one woman in Rome back in Claudius's time. My young drag queen looked lovingly at the $20.

"Think of it as a tip and a tribute to your loveliness," I said, taking a fingernail to the underside of his cock. He had been cut, probably born in some urban hospital where baby boys were marked civilized at birth. I winced thinking of how much that must have hurt, wrapping my hand around the base of his cock, moving my hand so that the little finger could play on the skin between the balls and his asshole.

He liked it. I started the slow nibbling tease on the line where the foreskin had been cut away. He was sweating, pumping. I was curled up on the floor working on him, my own cock moving again, trapped under my left leg, though. If I played this right, I could get another blowjob out of him.

Sploosh. Okay?

I stood up and pulled off the rest of my clothes, then started undressing him, but this frightened him. He pulled the pantyhose up and the skirt down. "You want to fuck me?"

"I'd like to see you completely naked. I'm completely naked. There's so much more to play with when you're completely naked."

He was embarrassed because he had extra nipples below the usual ones. I didn't care, more points for pleasure. I had them, too. His people must have a strain of the old blood, I thought. We kneeled on the bed and fenced with our cocks, laughing, not needing to be anything other than two bodies taking pleasure. He forgot to watch the $20 on the dresser; I forgot to worry about what he'd steal if I fell asleep on him. I closed my thighs on his cock when he was getting really excited. He should have learned to like that better — it would have helped him through the AIDS years. I put my fingers in his ass and pressed down on his prostate. Boom. Nice thing about the young boys is that they can keep going, but he looked like this had been enough. I pulled his legs together and got myself off between them, but without much cooperation from him. He tossed an arm back over his head and said, "You waste all your girls?"

I thought but didn't say that he looked like a boy to me, and I liked him better naked that way. "I treat people good."

"You could do well if you dyed your hair. Nobody'd think you were more than 18, tops."

"Thank you."

We walked back to the Stonewall together, my gold chains safe, the $20 I'd promised her in her pocketbook. I thought about adding another $100 for a better wig. "I'll dye my hair," I told him. "I want to look younger."

"I can't do this forever," she said.

I didn't tell her she could, because she couldn't.

"Judy Garland is dead," she said. "I'm in mourning."

I didn't have the same fetish for Garland, but I gave her a hug and said, "I didn't get your name."

"The Divine Miss Michelle," she said.

"Rhymes with mine," I said. "I'm Vel."

☞

Vel paused in telling the story. "Does this embarrass you?"

Carolyn said, "No, I've read the accounts. And at least you're not into golden showers and scat."

"Straight or gay, some women seem to dig hearing about man-with-man sex."

"We're trapped in the erotic," Carolyn said.

"No, I'm trapped in the erotic," Vel said. "As a woman, you're trapped in having consequences over it."

"That's not always true," Thomas said.

☞

But I should be telling this story as the story of the Stonewall Riots and not as an erotic story. The cleaned-up version of this story is that I met a female impersonator in a bar full of such people and males who courted them. She agreed to go home with me for a price. We consummated our deal and then put our clothes back on and walked into a riot. It was June 27, 1969, 1:20 a.m. If I give you a blow-by-blow description of everything, it's going to take us to well past midnight.

Miss Michelle saw cops walking into the bar, but it was later in the night than normal. Later, I heard all sorts of explanations for this raid, this time. People had been blackmailed into embezzling from banks; people had been rowdy. It had been about a century or two since I'd been beaten for loving men, so I'd forgotten how much it hurt.

The patrons refused to accept being rousted this time, whether they had IDs or not. Michelle rushed right in to join the other drag queens in telling the cops off. The cops grabbed a dyke, thinking she'd have fewer defenders here than the boys would have, but that didn't work. The cops and the queens were fighting in the street. I didn't know what I wanted to do. This wasn't the way queens were supposed to behave, though cops behaving this way was pretty typical in your puritanical ages. The cops were beginning to realize they were being beaten up by fake girls.

Michelle joined a line of other drag queens, kicking in a chorus line, singing

> We are the Stonewall girls
> We wear our hair in curls
> We wear no underwear
> We show our pubic hair
> We wear our dungarees
> Above our nelly knees

The cops looked like they didn't know whether to shit, shoot, or die. Memories of earlier beatings started bubbling toward the surface. I decided to get out and go back to my room in the Chelsea, no matter how historic this occasion might be.

A large man with semi-dark skin and somewhat black African features said, "the Mollies are finally kicking ass." He looked as though all this was bringing him to climax just watching.

I knew the Mollies. "Do you want to hang around and watch what happens, or do you want to get out of here?"

"I'm staying."

"Um, okay." I looked back at Sheridan Square and saw two drag queens sitting on a cop. Things like that made police types very angry in most times. I'd found a way to get a driver's license in New Jersey, which didn't require photographs, but wasn't sure what happened to people who didn't have ID in this era. I walked on imitating the butchest straight man I'd ever known, a peasant weaver turned military contractor named Sforza. The cops grabbed a straight folk singer named Dave van Ronk and let me walk out of there.

The next day, after I'd dyed my hair, The Divine Miss Michelle showed up at my room in the Chelsea, high as a high creature on marijuana—bruised, giggling, still chanting the drag queen national anthem. She'd gotten a new wig, probably dropped when someone with more to hide yanked it off and ran to her car to become the banker in a bespoke suit, if Americans then had bespoke suits.

"Wow. You look so much younger now. Wow. I am so glad we got back for the riot. The queens will change the world."

"At least New York," I said. Yes, it changed New York, began the whole move toward greater acceptance of same-sex love, but the drag queens ended up being still left in the kitchens and dining rooms of the world: class and race trump orientation in most cultures. But she was so happy now. I shucked the female stuff away and got a giggling Hispanic boy in my hands and made him very happy in the discreet version of this story, and fucked him silly by sitting him on my cock and stroking his cock along the whang string in the more graphic version of this story.

He put back on the female identity and said, "Come back to the Village with me."

"Darling, I'm afraid of the police."

"I fuck the police," she said, pumping an arm up militantly, nails all shiny with red polish. I shrugged and pulled on my running shorts and a nylon singlet. This was a nice time to be in — rowdy enough so that I forgot most of the past and my age. The Divine Miss Michelle and I took the elevator down, and she turned her way while I ran up to Central Park to run around the lake, feeling like a body not in any particular time. Couple of men eyed me and I eyed them back: yes, but not right now. I looked at the ducks in the lake and thought how tasty they'd be split and grilled over a fire. As horses under riders passed on the bridle trail, I wondered how many of these civilized horses even thought the first person on their backs could be a predator. Kids were flying kites while guys from Trinidad played steel drums, the sound track for the day. I was an archaic pair of eyes watching all this and thinking how extraordinary it was, then sank into the moment and just ran, high on what I would learn were beta-endorphins.

Later at a more discreet bar, I made it with a poet in the back room toilet. He didn't tell me whether he was famous or not, and I wouldn't have known he was a poet if one of the other guys standing around hadn't told me. He was blond, a bit older, and a really good kisser. Then I ran into the black guy who'd mentioned the Mollies.

The day was lots of fun. Everyone at the bar talked about Stonewall; how they'd never put us back in the closet now, but that the drag queens sometimes were giving straight people the wrong idea about what it meant to be a gay man in America. I nodded to indicate that I heard them.

A couple of days passed. The riots didn't stop with the first night, but the city started having dialogues with the responsible members of the gay community, whoever they were.

On Saturday, The Divine Miss Michelle turned up out of drag, in a Grateful Dead tee shirt and jeans, looking distraught. "My family kicked me out of the house. I didn't even get arrested, but they heard. Bunch of gossips. Can you come with me to get my clothes?"

I didn't want him moving in with me. I travel light. And if he'd been weeping, I'd have felt it was more a scam, but he looked truly lost. I hated to think that I was the first person to have been kind to him, but the other alternative was that he saw me as a sugar daddy. I knew I was better looking than he was, too, and with the dyed hair could beat him at the lady man whore game. If I wanted to.

So we stood there for a moment. He knew not to ask for more. I was wondering how generous I felt. "I can go with you to get your clothes and take them somewhere — you have a friend — else."

"Ah, man, you don't have to. I can get someone else to help me."

I wondered about that. If he had someone else, wouldn't he have gone there first? Or did I just look like the richest person he knew? If I sold one of the Klines or a small Klee, I could do a lot for him, but I hadn't wanted to do that yet. I had to get my NJ drivers license renewed and find another dead baby so I could get a birth certificate with a date that didn't look like I'd borrowed my father's driver's license. But why should I do anything for him? And was he luring me uptown to be robbed? "I'll hold on to your stuff until you get a new apartment. You do work, don't you?"

"I'm a cook," he said. "I just don't have the down payment, security. And I don't have ID."

"Oh." He said he was from Puerto Rico, which meant he was legally a US Citizen. But I was beginning to understand the difference between the various Hispanic immigrants to the United States. We got in a cab.

"They changed the locks. They've got all my clothes."

"They've probably thrown out the drag clothes if they're that mad at you. Are you sure they'll be home? Michelle, what can I call you in front of them?"

"Mario. My father is Huaman Campos."

And I'd slept with his grandfather several centuries removed or someone like him. That sounded like an Andean name. "From Puerto Rico."

"I thought so," Mario said. "That's what he told me."

Ah, fuck. First, yes, he was turning to me because I was the richest-looking friendliest person around. I shouldn't have paid him. I could have blown him for fun and turned and walked out of the bar that night. He was cute, and this wasn't the easiest age to be a young poor gay boy, though AIDS made it worse before it got better.

And the AIDS years, that I'd skipped hiding out in China as the perfect Eastern barbarian sex maniac, were right in front of him.

Young and dumb and full of come. I wanted to give him the big lecture about condoms and drugs, but he would think I was talking about clap and syphilis, which tend to be visible. All the parasites, too. I'm immune, but I can distribute if I'm not careful.

I couldn't tell him not to get as much pleasure as he could, but if he was Andean, he wasn't going to be as resistant to AIDS as the Europeans whose ancestors had gone through the plague and lived. He had to be part European, though, with his face.

"I travel a lot," I said. "I'm not staying here long." I'd come here to see some people I'd met in 2001, when we were celebrating the right beginning date of the new century. I hadn't started to look them up yet, but this is Mario's story. He's the darkest of the three queens in the vid. You saw it, the almost insect-like faces with belled skirts swarming out of the castle.

And so we came to the apartment building, and I waited while he ran the buzzer and begged his father to let him in. The father finally let him in. We walked up the stairs, and I decided this wasn't about me being robbed.

Mario's father was Andean. I ventured some Ayamara, and he flinched and said in stiff Spanish, "We were born in Puerto Rico." His wife was fairer-skinned, Spanish. Probably they'd run out of Peru just ahead of her daddy.

"You don't want Mario living here anymore. Is there a reason?"

Campos looked anguished, not contemptuous, though he obviously figured out how his son had managed to get a patron. I wondered if he had been the boy-love of some older man in his youth. So many men pass through loving boys, being loved as a boy. I was well ahead of my time for mostly lusting after people who...ah...appeared at least to be my own age. I suppose I'm the ultimate hebephile. He finally said, "People talk. The police were chasing him."

I said, "But they didn't catch him. Does he need papers?"

Boy, that was unsubtle. Everyone looked down at the floor. I didn't know why they'd left Peru or Bolivia, or how this man who appeared to recognize Ayamara got to New York City, how close they'd lived to Lake Titicaca. If he was a highlander, perhaps his Spanish wife couldn't bear children in the heights.

"Perhaps I was too rash," Campos said.

His wife looked blonder and more pissed off. This wasn't the usual way parents were supposed to act, but some tribes in the deserts of Peru and Chile had made the Incas gibber with nightmares of cock and come being wasted, so I'd found those tribes around Titicaca. Those people had been most gracious and accommodating. They weren't beautiful people, not really my kind, but sometimes being around natural beauty, good cloth, and great festivals made up for less than thrilling visual sexual stimulation. Mario had Daddy's darkness and Mom's Spanish skinny ass. She finally said, "I was punished for marrying you, first to lose a child, then to bear a faggot." There's a different word for that in Spanish, and she used it, but meant the ugliness.

I could tell that their different ideas about their son were abrading the love between the two. The family photographs showed another son in the shots. I wondered where he was today. I'd ask Mario later, but maybe they'd all be happier if he was out of the house. They wouldn't have to worry about Immigration or think about Mario. I didn't want to stake him to anything he couldn't afford (I was going to leave him after all), but I could find him something he could afford on cook's wages and at least get him into a lease.

Rent-stabilization was going to affect some of the cheaper apartments between the East Village and the old Village, then those would be gentrified and he could sell out the apartment rights or stay there, if he lived through the AIDS years.

We got his clothes packed up into two suitcases and a couple of garbage bags and took a cab back to my room at the Chelsea. A couple of phone calls later, I found him an apartment for $120 a month on Mott Street north of Houston. The neighborhood looked like shit then, but I remember seeing it in 2001 when the trees that some people were going to plant had grown up. The apartment had a kitchen that was the hall to the bathroom and a foyer that we could turn into a tiny dining room. He had tacky, drag-queen taste, but I found him two nice leather covered writing tables at the junk shop across Houston, then took him to eat at John Bellato's. He'd never had Northern Italian cooking before. I hoped he could become a better cook, one that could actually make a decent living, but I didn't want to pay for that.

Even though I kept my room at the Chelsea, I helped him scrounge for street furniture for the flat, getting a desk here and a bookshelf there. We went up to the Strand where a strange punk woman poet worked while taking workshops at the New School and bought him a collection of conversation pieces. I wondered if he had any real talents besides the lust for a good time, but that would be enough for the next couple of years. And maybe he'd figure out how to survive beyond that, or not. He would have been happier in those Peruvian desert kingdoms before the Incas showed up.

He taught me to appreciate drag, though. You'd have thought in 14,000 years, I'd have gotten it before, but no. Developing that gender-fuck thing is hard in loin cloths and leggings. I'd been a guy with a taste for other guys. That didn't make me a chick since I couldn't show vulva framed in a string skirt. Society has to be further along for that particular spin on same-sex attraction. We were all pretty naked in a lot of ways back when, except in the winter when we were all bundled up in furs. But even in furs, we were barer brained than people became later.

Vel stopped.
Thomas asked, "What happened to him?"
"I haven't had the heart to find out."
"Why don't you?"
"Don't want to wreck the memory.
He was a beautiful boy."

Blonde and Ivory

I don't know if this was in England or in country now under the North Sea. My sister wasn't with us for this trip, just the people who'd come to manhood and womanhood in the spring: Flat Nan, Ro, Ken, Jev, Ann, and me. The foreign boy had been hurt and was with the old men knapping flints. These aren't the names we had then, just names that I tag them with when I tell family about my past. Modern names keep them from being too exotic. They were just people to me.

Ro and I had been together for a while; Jev and Flat Nan were more or less thrown together from ill luck. He'd have wanted someone with more tits; she'd have wanted more tits if she could have had them, but she had more than the last summer even though her baby hadn't lived. Ann was the queen, the first blonde in our parts, who was supposed to be for Ken's father but who'd taken up with Ken instead. We'd traded one of our girls for her somewhere to the cold, nearer the ice than where we were now. She had the languages of the cave painters, the ivory bead makers, the people who drove horses over cliffs. And she was blonde with blue eyes — a scary little woman in some ways, beautiful in others. The women in our group first thought she was blind, an albino, but she wasn't. She knapped the skin knives like no other woman, drilled beads, had a neat hand with a hole punch on hide and a deft hand with a needle, following the trace of holes.

And she'd been traded like jewelry through at least six tribes before we'd gotten her, though she hadn't talked much about that before this hunting trip. She hated everyone who'd traded her, but learned what she had to learn to be valuable.

We were wading through wet snow with all our jewelry on and in leggings, furs, and hats, walking and sliding in shoes made for dry snow. Ro and I were Ken's honor guard, safe allies because we weren't competition. Neither of us was a full man-woman with the skills of a woman and a man's strength. We were goofy demi-guys who could fight.

The mammoths left their usual huge spoor through the snow, big tracks, the bigger spots where they'd dug up grass and lichen to eat. We moved slowly for a day or so, not wanting to share all the meat, hide, and ivory with the rest of our group, the yellow dogs slinking around behind us. We saw the mammoths, three of them, one old guy with his left tusk all broken and his trunk scarred by lions or bears, probably defending a calf. The two others were females, smaller tusks, no babies running at their sides. Maybe they were all too old to breed, last of their kind here. The mammoths dumped their shit and ran, knowing our kind from their own memories.

The dogs circled around, then went low-bellied, slinking as though we might spear them instead of the mammoths. Ann said, "There's a creek a mile away that direction. They'll bog down in that if they don't remember it's there."

The dogs watched us fan out and picked their own spots in the line as though they'd understood Ann. Ken waved from one end. I waved from the other. We both carried the spear-throwing sticks the Americans would later call atlatls, something that the oldest man I ever met knew as something from the mountains with the bi-colored bison. And we all carried heavy poking spears and feathered darts for the atlatls. If the mammoths charged, they'd be more likely to go through where the dogs were, dogs being only able to bite close up.

The dogs watched us, then the mammoths. The mammoths stopped moving and went flank to flank, looking at us. We slowed down and began clanging the darts against the spears on the side opposite of the way we wanted them to go. They looked at us, heads swinging. Meat thinking. The old male began walking toward us, swinging his trunk. The two females moved together, maybe crying for him, brushing the snow off each other's backs as it began falling. He fanned his ears, so much like human jug ears sitting out sideways I almost laughed, but he was staring straight at me. I notched a dart in my atlatl. They knew about the creek and weren't going to run that way and be bogged down. We couldn't take them all. They couldn't take us all, so the old male was going to kill me or die trying. I was angry that he'd decided I was the weakest end of the chain, but Ken was some bigger than I was, fully six foot and a half, and meaner and more male-smelling than I was.

He's coming the oldest mammoth, broken tusk and all, moving slowly, eyes fixed on mine. Bastard. Maybe this time, I lose. I waited until he got closer and slammed a dart into his trunk. He squealed from the pain. I tried for his eyes. The dart went high, into the spongy skull skin.

I jumped sideways even before it was necessary, shitting myself. Another dart hit the old bull from the side. His female friends were running off with a young male dog chasing them, yapping stupidly. I put the stabbing spear against the ground and told the bull, "You might get me, you bastard, but it's going to cost you."

The bull sighed hugely, two more darts in his sides. I could smell blood on his breath, feel his breath, smelled shit and blood, him with the darts in his lungs. He slowly reached out with his trunk and touched the stabbing spear. I was looking at his eyes, full of tears. "We need to eat," I said. "Please die for us."

He turned and began walking toward the woods. We knew he'd taken enough darts to the lung to kill him, and we didn't push him to bleed him out. The two cows had gone out away from the creek and the woods, away from us. He'd sacrificed himself for them, but they were already too old for calves.

I took off my leggings and breech clout and cleaned up the piss and shit as best I could with snow, then dressed again in the wet mess and ran after them: the group with an old dying mammoth in front; dogs yapping at him from a respectful distance; Ro, Jev, and Ken behind the dogs; and the two women behind them. The blood grew thicker and thicker as the old bull's muscles twitched the darts in his lungs. He turned and charged again, but blindly, then raised his trunk, smelling for us. My spear to his head had gotten blood in his eyes. Ken looked carefully, raised his atlatl and put a dart in the other eye, then jumped sideways, fast, as the old bull turned. *Meat, be meat for us.* I said to the bull, "The hurting will stop if you die now."

The bull heard my voice and maybe recognized it, or my smell, and turned away from us and walked for a few more steps before brushing off the darts in his side against a tree. Then he brushed away the darts still hanging from his other side and the one in his head. He began to try to brush out the one Ken had put in his eye, but that probably hurt too much. We started chanting, "The hurting will stop if you die now." He lay down, but we didn't trust this and waited until Ann said, "if you wait too long, he'll rot inside." Ro and Ken took the stabbing spears and stuck the bull in his neck. The heart blood wasn't pumping. We all jumped up and down, cheering, and began cutting the hide off, thanking him for dying near trees so we could make a cord from some of the hide and stretch the rest of it for splitting. The dogs came forward for innards when we paunched him, and I washed in his gall before cleaning myself up with snow. We built a fire, and I took off my breech clout and went to the creek to wash it, shivering, then went back to slide on the ribs and warm myself in the body cavity while my clothes dried near the fire. When Ro crawled into the body cavity, I was naked and slick with fat. We giggled and fucked in the flesh cave. I was deliriously happy not to have been squashed into a blood-and-bone pulp by the bull whose body we were honoring with our joy. The bull would live on in us and in the yellow dogs, not in flies and beetles.

When my clothes were dry, the mammoth was cooling, so we packed the insides with snow while the dogs ran off and buried what they hadn't gorged on. Stupid dogs, we weren't coming back here again. Not that many centuries later, the whole place would be under water, if it was where I think now that it was. But so much has changed.

We moved all the mammoth parts off the main body hide. As the men cut the flesh off the bones and then split the flesh further, the women cut the ivory out of the beast's skull and then used a flint flake to saw it into chunks we could carry back to camp. The bad tusk we left behind. We had the brains for supper, and then Ann had us clear away the rest of the mammoth from the hide. We put it flesh-side against the snow and folded it over all of us and slept between the wool and hair, itchy but warm. The dogs woke us up in the morning by pulling bits off the hide. We chased them off and laid out the hide fur-side down. The women began cleaning off the last bits of flesh and fat while we cut off part of the hide to build a frame for further dressing and splitting of the hide. Ann took a leg hide and made a neat water boiler out of it, heating stones in the fire we'd made the night before and dropping hot stones in the water. We ate boiled stomach with the greens inside for breakfast and lunch, splitting the remaining meat and building a smoking rack out of the greenest wood we could find.

Ann told us how to build a seat for her and Flat Nan, so they could work their way down the mammoth hide, splitting it. One side would be a robe, the other mammoth suede, boot top, boot soles where it was thickest on the shoulders.

"Now, be quiet while we're working," Ann said. Women — always something fiddly they had to have silence for. The men and dogs sat around feeding the fire, splitting or stealing meat, hanging the meat out of dog-jump range to dry. The dogs were still stupidly burying what they couldn't put in their stomachs. The women cut downward, Ann checking Nan's work with the half round splitting knife, pulling the suede down away from the fur side. It took almost all day to split the hide, then we had to pull out the long hairs for cord making and dress the hides in the brains we hadn't eaten and smoke them, then soften them so the women or one of us could pack them back to where the rest of the group was.

Ann and Nan were exhausted from the fiddly work. We dug a ground pit with shovels cut from the mammoth's shoulder bones, then another one, tiring ourselves out. The now thinner mammoth furry side of the hide still kept us warm for the night. Tomorrow, we'd set both hide halves up to smoke, dig another shelter pit for us and use the ribs and other bones for support and turf the thing over. It wouldn't be as warm as we might like, and we couldn't sleep in the mammoth robe again until it was cured, but we'd done well. We ate more mammoth meat; the dogs went out and ate some of what they'd buried since we were defending the cache from them now.

Ann lay between Ken and me. The soft breasts pushed against me. I shrugged. "You really prefer Ro?" she whispered.

Yeah, especially when Ken's listening on your backside, I thought. "Yes, but I do think you're oddly beautiful, just not for sex."

Ken chuckled. Ann turned back to him. I was too tired for anything anyway and still was trembling inside from having almost been killed by this mammoth. I got the odd feeling that the old bull had decided to let me live, could see something about me that I didn't know yet.

When I woke up, I put on an extra tunic that someone had brought and went out to clean my breech clout more carefully. I could dry it in the smoke pit. We draped one hide suede-side on a frame over the first pit, then moved some of the coals in with one of the bone shovels. Over the next several days, we dried meat, smoked the hides, ate, fucked, got fucked.

Ann made ivory beads most of one day, almost five hands of beads, twenty-four probably, each taking about a quarter of an hour as measured by a now-time clock. She strung the beads on a mammoth hair cord and gave them to Ken. They glowed against his skin. I thought she'd look particularly good herself in gold beads, but we weren't near where gold lumps could be pulled from the streams. Or amber. I wanted my own ivory beads, but didn't think Ken would let her make them for me. Or perhaps he would.

When I asked her to teach me how to make beads, she looked at me, a sad look actually, as though I'd reminded her of someone she'd lost in all the trading I didn't know about yet. "Sure, you might as well learn women's skills, too. It's your way, isn't it?"

"Ro and I just fell into this."

"No tribal custom."

"We've heard about other people doing things like we do."

"I thought boys had to be turned into man-women like girls are turned into trade girls."

"We figured out we liked each other. Nobody seemed to mind."

"You are so cute. Your people could trade you to some men."

"I'm happy with Ro. People think we're a little silly, but we're good brothers."

She said, "I'll teach you."

"And spinning," I said.

"Ooo, you really don't know how insulting that is," Ann said. "You'd be stealing our stuff."

"Just the beads, then."

Ann showed me how to cut the ivory two ways: with string and grit, which took a while, or with a flat flint flake and prying, which was faster but messier. Then, I'd use a gritty stone to round the bead, and put a hole in the bead by drilling with bone fragment and wet sand. It was routine work after I got the hang of it, so I began cutting out little dicks and balls. The anthropologists have never found those, but they've found thousands of the other kinds of ivory beads.

"I hate you all," Ann said when we'd both finished a bead at the same time and paused. "And I hate being a freak."

"Why? People love your hair, the skin is also very fashionable."

"Everyone wants me. Everyone becomes scared of me, so they trade me off. Six times."

"If you'd stop being scary, they'd stop trading you off, maybe."

"I'm lying to you."

"I don't care."

"I'm not lying to you. I know how to be scary, knew it even as a little girl. I could tell when people were going to die and start making grave goods for them."

"I can see what's coming, too," I said.

"Oh?"

"Yeah." I didn't know if I should tell her more. "I could be just as scary as you, but it would hurt my friends."

"What's scary?"

"You're going to grow old with us, wrinkle up," I said. "Nobody's going to trade you away ever again." I could see her older self with a son, egging the son on into challenging his father, Ken, the future older Ken. And I could hear her complaining that I wasn't getting older. Everyone else was, and I wasn't. And I could see the son, once he was head of the tribe and had sired children with one of my sisters, decide thoughtfully that she'd been angry long enough and that she would be out of pain if she were dead, just like the mammoth we killed three days ago. And...

I couldn't tell her this. She'd have some pleasure in her life with her children if she didn't know what was coming.

After the hides were cured, we walked back to the meeting place and waited with our hides, ivory, and bone tools for the others to come back from their hunts. Both women had gotten enough fat to conceive, and we had more babies in the summer, with lots to eat even after we'd gone through the mammoth we'd killed and the several reindeer and horses it took to get us through the winter. The salmon ran up the rivers and creeks in the spring as they'd done for millions of years before us. The mammoth cows found a male who was fertile and capable and had two more calves, so mammoths weren't extirpated yet where we were, though we'd kill one of the cows winter after next.

And I didn't grow old though everyone else did, but we so rarely reached extreme old age in those days that most people didn't notice.

I stayed with Ro even as he aged. He died in his sleep one night, which I'd seen coming for decades and had been upset with until I realized how nice not dying in vast pain was.

My sister's children were grown men then, and I took care of my sister's children's children even when we had to move to what would be France to escape the ice closing in again. One time, centuries later, someone traded me off as a woman man, but I came back after he died, as I'd seen he would die, and made myself useful again, as I have always been useful to my family. My loves live happily ever after, for a while.

Very Minor God in Real Flesh

After the Romans, I lived in a niche cut into chalk by a spring bubbling out of a hill. Both the spring and I were sacred because the spring never dried up and I always had food. The people around accepted that I could disappear and come back with food, with rabbits and pigeons and wheat bread. I kept the occasional stolen pizzas for myself and entertained myself with a series of hungry young men. I don't really know where the spring was or how long I stayed there; it could have been fifty years or five hundred. Some people had old coins with Anthony and Cleopatra on them, so somewhere in the Roman-touched world, which meant anywhere from the Indus to Somerset.

The weather was slightly chilly, slightly dry, and people changed what they wore from tunics over loincloths to breeches, but I wore loinclothes, leggings, and whatever shirts I could persuade people to trade me for food under a fur coat that I had sewn of ermine, knowing it would become the fur royalty claimed later. Life was pleasure. I had a supply of hashish that I got when I time-jumped to visit a boy brothel in Istanbul and smoked a fair amount of that, and drank the local barley ales, and brought in the local boys. I'd found a niche in the chalk where I could stay a god forever, I thought. I taught the boys a few words of Latin, which could melt into any tongue brought in later.

Then one day, a man with silver and gold throat armor and gold-wired cuffs on his gloves, a band of gold around his head, all scruffy and dusty now, came up to claim the spring. He rode with maybe two dozen mounted archers dressed in leather pants with felted coats caked with dust, who surrounded him, bows with arrows nocked and pointing at the villagers. I would have gone home, or jumped to another time, but I felt that the spring and I were equally sacred and that he wasn't. I'd been a minor god for so long, and the hash had curled most of my past memories right out of my brain, which was very comfortable.

So, there the minor king was, and there I, the minor god, was. He sat on his horse with his dirty scratched gold looking at me; I sat in my niche looking back at him. His interpreters tried the local language, but I'd never bothered to learn it since the silent trade had been working so well for so long, food for boys. I shrugged. They tried another language. I'd known it somewhere, but not in precisely that form. I spoke back in the sort of country Latin I'd learned from the Romans who'd been in Somerset. One of his interpreters knew a better kind of Latin than I did and explained that his king wanted to know what I was and whether I claimed the land here.

Sounding like a rustic, I told them I was the god of this spring.

The king, who appeared to know that kind of Latin even if he couldn't speak it, nodded at me, a polite minor-god-warrior-king-to-minor-agricultural-god sort of nod. He was riding in stirrups, I remember now, invented in the east some centuries earlier, when the Persian Empire decided the world was a battle between the forces of Light and the forces of Darkness. How he'd gotten on this chalk down and even where the chalk down was, I haven't been able to figure since—anywhere from France to England though I don't remember a boat ride between here and Somerset, or even how I got home for Yules.

He and his men had ridden hard through the smashup of the Roman Empire and were now tired and ready to claim a kingdom and clean their jewelry and gold-crusted battle gear.

"Is this the only good spring on the hill?" the interpreter asked me.

"I don't know more than the village and the downs." The villagers ran sheep on the hill above the spring, raised wheat and barley in the chalk-stream basin.

The king looked at me as though I was a simpleton and asked something, eyes on me, waiting for the translator. "What do you do for them?"

"I keep them from going hungry if the crops fail. If raiders steal their sheep."

The king smiled slightly. He spoke again to the man who knew Latin. They discussed what the king was going to say. "How do you keep them from starving?" The king was being stingy with his questions.

I visualized a sheep pasture, stepped over and nicked a suckling lamb, one of twins, then stepped back with the lamb in my arms. Back in the future, a sheepdog was barking furiously, but the scene faded. I handed the lamb up to the king, who motioned for his translator to take it. They camped at the spring that night, roasting the lamb, looking down rather than catching me in the eyes. All looked down except the little black-haired king, his gold circlet off as his face was being shaved by one of his archers.

He watched my eyes as I looked at the various men eating, their two camp women moving among them in men's clothes but with breasts under that. I looked back at him to see who'd blush first.

He smiled. I looked away first. I went back to my niche in the hill and waited to see who'd follow me into the chalk.

The little king did. I wondered if he'd ever smoked hash and if he would. I prepared a pipe and lit it, inhaling smoke, then offered it to him, motioning. He took the pipe and sniffed. If he could recognize that smell, he could have come from a long way off. Holding the pipe but not smoking, he smiled slightly as the hash hit my brain. He knew enough Latin to say, "Tall God, you prophesy?"

"No," I said. "Not on the smoke." I couldn't see when I was stoned.

He said, "The fire in this is cooling."

"I can fix that." I had an oil lamp burning in a niche that stained the chalk all golden. "Call it a pipe."

"Smoke wine."

"How far did you come from?"

"Very far. We here now. We will keep the sea by us."

"All I want is not to have my boys stop coming. I have a taste for them."

He held out my pipe. "Drink smoke more."

"Oh, no, you smoke with me."

"God of Spring. I will not hurt you."

"You're littler than I am. You can't hurt me."

"Drink more smoke. Then I will drink smoke."

I inhaled and held a splinter of wood into my oil lamp and lit the hash while he smoked it. Such a cute little king. He pulled his mouth off the pipe and smoke poured out his mouth as he coughed. Words in his own tongue brought in two friends to turn me belly down.

I said, "If you'd use some of the oil in the flask, I'd be happier and it would be easier for you."

"I am a man. If you are a god, get out of their hands."

"Just use the oil." My standard silicone lube, anachronistic as ever. Everyone was getting extremely aroused. I hoped he wasn't planning to bring in the whole gang. That would be a pain in the ass even for me. "In the clay bottle below the niche with the lamp."

"Clown," he said, meaning rustic. His eyes unfocused a bit as the hash hit him and he shook his head as though that would shake the smoke out. "Drink some more smoke?" he asked, holding me the pipe while his men still held me down.

"I will if you promise to use the oil in the jar. Remember I will not respect you for this."

"You will," he said, but he held the pipe stem to my mouth and played a wood splitter over the hash while I drew in as large a lungful as I could with two men pressing me against the floor.

"Can they let me alone? It's more fun if I'm willing."

He smiled and said something to the archers who took off my clothes before they let me up. So I was going to be screwed and tattooed, or branded. Or just made property of the king, his pet subordinate god. I sat in tailor position.

"Kneel, kiss." His dick was out, but he still had his dirty throat armor on. I was just stoned enough to find the scene erotic and funny at the same time, but a sober part of my brain told me I should fight this. The kinglet in the dirty gold would be bones before I cut new teeth. Why fight it? I had all the time in the world to play with him. I knelt and kissed his cock — uncircumcised, so too early for Islam and not Jewish.

His hips rocked twice, then he walked over and brought the lube back, too turned on to think about what it felt like as he poured it in into his hands. I ran my fingers down the muscles in his belly, trying to get him to ejaculate before he turned me over. His two men were watching as though they'd seen him rape people before but not with foreplay. Finger under his cock, behind the foreskin, on the little ridge there. He hissed and pushed me down and rolled me over and stuck his siliconed fingers up my anus. I arched on my knees and elbows, my own erection slapping me in the belly. Now he teased me, fingers playing around trying to get me even more aroused.

One of the archers suggested in Latin worse than mine, "Beg king fuck you."

I tried to say, "Is that how this scene runs?" But the words fell out a mumble.

"He's forgotten his words," the king said. "He's mine." His cock rammed into my asshole and I gripped and he rode and I bucked, and felt him against my cock root and we hit a rhythm and came, him in me and me on the chalk floor. He pulled out and stood up. As I lay curled on the floor, he said, "Drink more smoke?"

I rolled over on my back and waved weakly. "No." I looked nervously at the archers who seemed to be pretty aroused by now. If hash kept me pinned in this time, I really needed to stop smoking hash.

The king said, "You are mine." He said something to the archers and they grumbled but left. I felt grateful that this wasn't going to be more of a scene than I wanted to handle. I also wanted to top the king as soon as possible. "Walk with me to the spring to wash."

I started to put on some clothes, but he said, "Naked. You have nothing to fear. You are mine."

He could call back the archers and drag me out kicking and screaming. My head was still so full of hash that my vision was off and all this looked like a vid. I walked out dripping with his semen and mine. The villagers were there by now, watching their god become the property of an alien king.

I waded into the spring and washed myself off. The king pushed my head under in a mockery of baptism. Then I walked back to my niche and he followed me in and dried me off and let me get dressed again.

Then he brought me down to the fire, cut off the tip of my left little finger just below the nail, and burned the stump with a hot spear point. I was so shocked I didn't scream.

"I eat of your flesh," he said, popping the tip of my finger into his mouth and swallowing nail, flesh, bone.

The villagers sucked in their breaths and waited for me to strike the king dead, but I was curled around my wounded hand, thinking that the flesh would grow back in the miracle of the next month or so, and show the king. The pain burnt the hash out of my brain, and I tried focusing on other times to jump to, but the pain kept me from focusing, too.

The king, having aroused me, raped me, and maimed me, had no further interest in me. My getting food for the villages was the act of his slave. The king married the local headwoman after defeating her husband in single combat.

I thought I'd grow the fingertip back, nail and all. But it grew back smooth. If I hadn't been a useful thief bringing him other time's foods, I suspect he would have had ordered me killed.

And nobody stopped me when I walked away and kept walking and walked all the way back to Somerset to home, knowing whatever I was, I could be hurt.

Centuries Ago and Very Fast

His present lover asked, "Why did you move to the chalk downs away from your family?"

Vel said, "It was easier than being at home unable to stop shit from happening there."

Blue as Neon but More Stiff
[Thomas's Story]

Vel and I lived quietly in the country and I liked it quiet when I wasn't on duty.

Off in a shed on Vel's farm, I found an old David Brown tractor, a little red jobbie, that dated back to sometime in the 20th Century, caked with mud and body a bit rusted. I found the online clubs dedicated to fixing them up, bought parts and appropriate paint, sanded out the rust with an angle grinder (Vel had all the tools from now to the Paleolithic) and began working on it, planning a really big garden for the next spring.

Vel tracked me to the shed a day or so after I got a delivery of parts off the Internet. As I put in the new distributor and adjusted the points, he stood in the doorway watching. He wore leather leggings, a soft leather tunic over a long linen shirt that came down to his thighs, one leg crossed over the other, right toes to the ground in front of the left foot, barefoot. I had absolutely no idea what period that dress was from, probably a mix of his favorite eras.

The valves didn't appear to need regrinding—someone, probably Vel, had bought this tractor new and not used it much.

I said, "You're quite the collector, aren't you? This tractor doesn't look like it's been used that much."

"Oh, someone else wanted to use it." I must have flinched because he quickly added, "Family."

"I can still buy parts and attachments for it. The David Browns have a cult following, it seems."

"There's a grist mill that works off the power take off if you want to make flour or beer."

I'd found the gang and single plows and mower and rake attachments earlier. If I grew a lot of wheat, I should get an old combine, but for haying and vegetables, we were set. The tires needed to be replaced, but I got the engine to turn over, and we stood listening to it for a while before I turned it off.

"Would you mind if I make a big garden this spring," I said.

"I can help you. Agriculture isn't foreign to me." He touched the tractor. "I've driven this."

"I should have asked if it was okay, but..."

"I'm your domestic partner. It's fine. When we move the ponies, their present paddock would make a good spot."

"You've got lots of fruit and nut trees, too."

"Some of them we've had for thousands of years. Like the family—the present hazels came from the old hazels. I used to chase deer and mammoths away from them. The ponies didn't eat them, but the goats that came later did. The apples and pears are later." He stood a moment as if remembering, then asked, "Do you need anything more?"

"I found what I needed online. I'm good."

"I want to show you more of our heirlooms."

He'd already taken me through one of the old stone barns filled with relics, mostly Mesolithic. I put down the

oilcan and wrenches, cleaned off my hands as best I could
with a much-used rag, and followed him back further.

He got lost in his memories, touching this spear straight-
ener, that piece of mammoth tusk, those spear points, the
net that I'd never seen the like of anywhere else other
than carved on stone women's hair. I think he wanted me
there to keep the artifacts from drowning him in the past.
But he hadn't brought me here to see the Paleolithic. We
walked quickly through the Mesolithic, skipped Copper
and Bronze, and entered the Iron Age. He had set up a
warp-weighted loom with sets of family stones carved for
that maybe 3,000 years ago. The thread was fresh.

"Is anyone going to weave it off?"

"Me."

"How old are the weight stones?"

"As old as the Norns or Fates," Vel said, meaning not as
early as the netted hair cap. "I could teach you to weave."

I laughed. "You want me to be that versatile? I'm a cop."

Vel stood before the loom, hips cocked, arms and body
swaying to pull out the warp, bring through the weft, beat
the thread up. He wove about an inch before he asked me,
his eyes on the thread, his hands up around the thread but
not moving, "Were you ever forced?"

"Yes."

"Me, too, but I got over it. Did your forcing scar you?"

I wanted to ask how long ago, but that didn't really
matter. "If you had good experiences before..."

"I'm very considerate. If you can't, you can't." He
managed to sound disappointed without looking petty. He
opened the threads up again and put the stick with the
weft in the space between the warps, then let the threads
fall together. "I did have a wonderful time with my first
lovers, in many ways."

"I don't get much out of being a bottom," I said.

He picked up a chain and looked at it carefully. I noticed it had links connected to the main chain. "Roman, slave chain. We found it after we bought the property back. I don't remember a damn thing about it other than it makes me uneasy." He put it down with a clank of links hitting the display case. "If you don't want to try, I'm certainly not going to force you."

I could volunteer to let him find his own bottoms, but I didn't want that either. "If you think you can make me happier than the last guy, we can try."

"We'll go slow. A couple of weeks of butt play." He pulled out an ancient dildo. "Don't flinch, not with this. We'll start with my little finger, in a finger cot, with lots of lube."

"I'm not..." I was about to say, afraid, and was glad he interrupted me.

"Or we can start out really easy. A feather."

"Whatever you say, Vel." I was going to be embarrassed if he tickled my butt with a feather.

He pulled a piece of cloth out of one of the cases, held it to his nose and inhaled deeply. My dick twitched watching him in the dim light, his nose buried in an old faded piece of woad-blue cloak. "Do you remember that?"

"I remember the guy. Sorry."

"Don't be sorry. That's all that's left?" I had to ask.

"He used to wear it in the winter."

Centuries before I was born. I tried to imagine losing that many people I'd been close to, realized I probably couldn't begin to.

Vel said, "I'm not going to look into our future. I'm not going to do anything except let you surprise me." His eyes were liquid in the cautious light selected to be safe for fragile antiques.

I found myself incredibly touched. "Thank you." We looked at each other and walked back to the house without saying more.

For a week, he just gently tongued along my butt, nothing going in. I started to relax finally, and found his tongue darting up my anus. He felt me tense up and pulled back and brought out the peacock feather that he'd threatened me with earlier. I rolled belly up and saw my flush down to my knees. He brushed my cock with the feather, then rolled the fingercot over his index finger, greased it with the lubrication he carried with him in all times, at all times, and blew me with his index finger pressing gently on my...my. I completely forgot what that was called as the blood ran from my blush to my dick. Ah, yeah, my outer sphincter.

Vel moved his chin up to my pelvis and locked eyes with me. The finger pressed around the ring. I tried not to tighten. Vel knelt up between my legs and said, "Is just the finger there okay?"

I nodded.

He pulled off the finger cot and went back between my legs with a warm washcloth to wipe away the lubricant. "Um."

"If you move to the edge of the bed and put your legs on my shoulders...."

I moved without thinking. His tongue began probing. It felt much better than that selfish bastard's dick had felt when I was 17.

Another week of just tongue and fingers. I started to feel silly. When I had my days off, I told him, "Let's go for it."

"I'm going to pull out if you're in the least bit of distress. I hope that's not what the other guy said. Okay, first you're going to douche with warm water whilst I put on a condom, a nice blue condom so it's not so scary. We're going to use warm lube. And we're going to go very slow."

I realize what a turn-on getting my butt was to him, but he was still being nice about it. We were about the same height, but I was heavier than he was if we ended up grappling.

In the bathroom, I unwrapped a head for the douche and got that in my butt without flinching. I took some extra time to pull back my foreskin and wash my dick in the sink. As I stood there naked, I heard Vel moving around in his bedroom, the fan of an electric heater coming on to take off any chill, then the condom wrapper being pulled off the condom, sounding like a candy wrapper being peeled off a mint.

Nervous as I imagined girls to be, I walked back in completely naked. Vel was lying on the bed with his erection sheathed in neon blue, a cushion under his back. "It's not latex, in case you react to that." He had his right hand working the lubricant up and down. "And blue to make it look smaller. Ready?" He smiled a quick v of lips, then pulled the lube out of the warming pot.

"Okay." I sat down on the bed, raised one hip so he could smear some of the lubricant on me, in me.

"You're going to kneel over my legs and work your way up. I'll let you do this at your pace. You'll still be on top."

I giggled slightly. Got over his cock and stopped, very puckered anus pressing lightly onto his dick. He took me and rolled me to his side, and just held me, stroking between my shoulder blades. "It's okay if you don't want to." I felt his chest hairs against my own that I didn't feel and realized he felt my own chest hairs against his in a mirror of the familiar ignored hair and the other's strange hair brushing skin and hair. He was sweating under the arms. He put his nose to my shoulder and breathed in deeply.

"Oh, come on," I said.

"We're going to stop here for a few minutes." His finger went around my sphincter. After about ten minutes, I could feel my sphincter surrendering. "Now." Words were getting hard. I moved back over his dick. He moved his hand down to guide me. He looked like he was trying very hard to think of something to keep from coming off before he got his dick up my butt. My butt just opened for him and I slid the rest of the way onto his hips. His eyes lost focus and he groaned slightly. My dick was floating over his belly, aching, being rubbed at the root deep inside me. I moved and found just the right place. He steadied me with his hands while his hips squirmed against the bed. I felt his hand flitter over my dick and I closed my eyes, just feeling him in me, me gripping him in waves, moving so cock root and prostate got...

Woom, I came all over his belly. He kept moving a bit more then came. I wondered what it would be like without the condom.

"Do I have to lift straight up?"

"Doesn't matter...now," Vel said, reaching down to hold the condom on his cock as I slid off him. He pulled it off and leaned up, shoulders sweat-sleek, to put it in a chamber pot under his bed.

We lay there cuddling, dozing off, and cuddling again. Vel murmured something in a language probably dead except for him. I nodded as though I understood, stroking down his far side from ribs to hip with the backs of my fingernails.

"Promised you that I wouldn't hurt you."

"More than okay."

He smiled as he went to deep sleep in my arms. I watched him for a few minutes before falling asleep myself. He was so beautiful sweaty. We woke up tangled in each other and got up to take showers and get dressed for breakfast. I felt like an ice splinter had been eased out of my soul, but I wanted to have him on my dick the next time.

"We need to fix up your room," Vel said. "Maybe install another bathroom in there with a douche in the toilet room instead of the bath." He bit his toast.

"Okay." I wondered if he wanted us to sleep apart when we weren't having sex, but somehow that didn't seem like him.

It took us about a week to fit a toilet with nice fixtures and Vel's plumbing specials into one of the niches. We knocked a hole in the fireplace and ran the waste pipes down and stack up that way, putting fireproof insulation around the pipes. Working with Vel on this brought us together beyond sex. We worked bare-chested and got nicked from stone chips the chisels set flying. Together we wrestled the toilet up the stairs, put in the wax ring, and fitted the toilet on top of that.

Vel said, "I love working with you," as we bolted the toilet down. "What kind of bed do you want?"

"If we're going to sleep together here rather than in your room, why not move your bed in here?"

"Okay," Vel said. "It's a lot to un-build, but okay."

I found out that the bed was put together with mortise and tenon joints, not a modern bed at all, and bigger than the doorway, so we did have to drill out some dowels and cut out some wedges and knock the thing apart with leather and rubber mallets. The bottom under the mattress was woven wood on a frame like a giant shallow basket turned upside down, no handles. I'd never seen anything like it and it didn't look over twenty-five years old.

"Better than bed slats and stronger than bed cords."

"You could use box springs," I said.

"We could make a flat frame and just put the box springs on top of that," Vel said.

We took the timbers for the bed frame across the landing into the new bedroom with toilet and bowl ensuite and put the bed together between a white-painted three-drawer chest we'd use for toys and a cupboard with wire ports for things we needed to heat. The wall warts ran along the wall connected by raw conduit. I wondered how old that wiring was. One conduit went up the wall and gave me a place for a ceiling fixture, wires and a gas pipe dangling down from a plaster ceiling medallion. We hammered the bed back together, next cut dowels and wedges and tightened the thing up again before dropping the bottom in place. Once we got the mattress in place and spread the sheets over it, we both collapsed on it.

"You want to test the toilet?" Vel said.

"No, why don't you test the toilet," I said, grinning.

I lay waiting with a bright red condom on my dick as Vel cleaned himself off for me. He came back into the room naked, unshowered but clean inside. "Unless you've been playing elsewhere, you don't need that now." He tried to unroll it but I didn't think it was going to come off now.

"Vel, just..."

He hopped on, already lubricated. "Give me your hand, he said. I raised my hand, already glad the condom was slowing me down some. He took my hand and leaned back hard and trusting, throwing one arm behind him gracefully, hand pointed as though he was making shadow birds. "Ah, Swan Lake."

"Err, Vel." His other hand was slippery, so I grabbed his wrist and then he gave me the other hand and we rocked and squirmed. I didn't need to touch him to get him off.

After I eased the condom off and threw it in the chamber pot, we rested, then he said, "You next. Bareback."

"We've got more to do to the room," I said.

"Yes. Install some trapeze rings and a flying harness," he said.

"Okay, I'll get up."

When I came back, he'd set two small pocket torches on the furniture on either side of the bed and closed the drape. He rolled back his foreskin, rubbed the lubrication on his dick and handed it to me. I rubbed some around my asshole. My nipples were tiny hard things all puckered. He touched them, ping, ping. I slid down onto him gently, my cock rising as his rubbed against the...stuff inside me. I could feel his skin against mine. He reached for my hands. I wondered if he could hold me, if I was flexible enough to bend backwards as he did. I propped myself up with one arm and gave him the other. He took my wrist. I tested his hold before I gave him my other hand. He was very strong. I was more limber than I thought I could be. We hung there, pinned with the throbbing, then he began humping against my weight, my weight on my knees and in his arms. Warm liquid. I tried to say something, couldn't speak at all. He kept pumping and blew through the air between us against my dick, his hands still holding me. I ground against him. He was still erect even though he'd come. I stopped thinking, closed my eyes and spurted all over his belly as though my eyelids coming down across my eyeballs were stroking my cock. He came again inside me, then eased me down beside him, a warm moist towel ready to wipe up.

"Um?" I said, feeling the towel go up between my buttocks.

"We've got towels, or you can go back and douche again."

"Towel." My bowels were quivering.

He said, "You'll smell of me for days." He raised his free hand to my face.

I began licking it. It tasted male. When I could put a few more words together, I said, "Thanks."

"Our pleasure," he said.

We went out the next morning and bought a recycled chandelier from one of Vel's fellow antique dealers, two women this time. I didn't know if they were family or not. And we bought another bed for Vel's room, just a plain bedsprings and mattress.

A day or so later, I decided to break the garden with the tractor plow. Vel helped me check the plow, which I thought I'd attached correctly following the instructions I'd gotten in email from one of the David Brown tractor fans. His hands ran over the lift and tested to make sure the coulters and plow points were still tight, then he nodded to me.

From net instructions and email, I plowed the field while Vel leaned against the paddock fence watching me. Plowing felt horridly Freudian, and I knew from his grin that he was thinking the same thing. I gritted my teeth and tried to concentrate on plowing straight rows, lifting the plow gang in the headlands, and cutting another row of three furrows. It was a small field, twelve turns, then I swiped across the headland nearest the gate, and stopped the tractor and got down and went up to Vel. He put his hands on my shoulders and began smelling me. I was sweating despite the weather, and the dirt had gotten into my hair. Vel found that particularly attractive. "My land on you," he said.

"Are you going to bury me here?"

He looked hurt, then annoyed. "Don't talk about that."

"Can you be faithful to me?"

He pulled back and looked at me, ancient eyes with a pity in them I was sorry to have called up. "Of course," he said. And I realized for him, my whole life wasn't more than a week. Of course, he could stay faithful to me as long as I lived. No big deal.

I'd lost a moment with him that could have been fun, rolling in the fresh plowed furrows, but as short as my life was to his, we'd have other moments. I got back on the tractor to put it up.

"See you back at the house," he said.

I drove the tractor to its shed and drained the compressor, then took the plow off the hitch and rolled it back by main force. And sat down and cried, not quite knowing for what. Dirt-streaked tears. I found as clean a rag as possible, and then remembered the faucet between the old paddock and the new and went back to it, cleaned away my self-pitying face and went back to Vel who was putting on wingtips. His suit jacket lay carefully across a chair back.

"I wanted to make sure everything was in order. I have to go to London tomorrow," he said.

I looked at him wearing the shirt, tie, and pants above the wingtips as cleanly and trimly as he wore tunics and leggings. What an elegant man. I helped him into the suit jacket, and then he walked upstairs to his own room and spent most of the night on the computer before coming to bed with me.

He took my hair and said, "Don't remind me of shit like death."

I nodded. Neither of us was ready for sex, so we just slept in the bed. In the morning, he frowned at the briefs he was putting on and then dressed with garters at the knees for his hose, the pants over that, the braces that I hadn't seen last night over the crisp cotton shirt that bagged in back, then the suit jacket and a long black overcoat over that.

"You look great," I said.

He kissed me and found his attaché case.

"Back tonight? Back tomorrow?"

"Tomorrow."

"Gay men selling antiques is such a cliché."

"I probably was the first," he said. I began dressing for work myself, hoping to have enough drunks to stay busy but nothing more than that. He said, "I'm with you now. That matters to me."

"It matters to me, too. Greatly."

He kissed me on the mouth and was out the door.

Work kept me busy, but not on edge. We busted a fence who tried to tell us she had no idea why anyone would have stolen things to sell to her shop and dealt with some idiot merging his Mercedes into a joke shop in Bath; then I went out to arrest someone who'd pounced on a waiter at a Balti place. Handling case files took up some time; after which I made a court appearance to get the assault case remanded to custody since he'd been beating on Pakis since 2002. A nice two days for a gay cop with a 14,000-year-old lover in Somerset.

Acid and Stoned Reindeer

The reindeer were stoned. Flat Nan, Ken, Ro, some other girls and a boy who'd just discovered sex, and I were chasing mammoths off the summer range so the horses could eat in peace and so we'd have some hazel nuts left for the winter. We didn't hunt mammoths until snow fell, which made tracking them like following a herd of Buicks. Mammoths always looked surprised when we found them, so I don't think they were that smart.

Centuries later, I was at a loft party in New York City, having gone back to see how some people I'd met in 2001 had gotten that way. It was easy to wrangle invitations to parties in the early 1970s if you were a presentable boy, and I've always been a presentable boy. The loft was full of painters with real gallery shows, of famous painters' future and present, and their ex wives and boyfriends, of the kinds of people who showed up to be at a party with famous painters, poets, and the various entertainments people who threw loft parties had to offer. Dancers danced. Painters chatted up art critics. Poetry professors chatted up graduate students past, present, and future. And I felt both in place and out of place, remembering parties in places that must have been Rome that felt like this or that could have been provincial capitals pretending to be as vicious as Rome. Clothes change; bodies and poses don't. I was maneuvering for the drinks table when someone said, "If you want to try acid, the punch is spiked."

If I was going to get drunk, I was going to be pinned down in time for the duration anyway, just like being asleep, so I might as well try something new. To lock me to the party time, I drank two big glasses of white wine, which was the screw-neck bottled cheap Chablis available at all bohemian parties those years. Then I took a drink of the punch. I'd heard about acid, like rye fungus without the fingers dropping off, and I was feeling reckless, which happens sometimes after you spend a couple of centuries being cautious after seeing a lover hanged. Stonewall marked the change; New York was full of possibilities those days. The revolution hadn't quite faded.

Even before the acid hit, I'd spotted a couple of guys who liked what they saw. And saw one man who'd lost his old lover and who would lose his young lover to AIDS, but this isn't that kind of story, so we've got to move on.

I knew not to spend too much time with the people who'd wonder why I didn't recognize them in 2001, so I found a couple of people who I knew would have moved away by then, two women, one also tripping and sitting in a chair while people worried about her, which amused her, the other curled up on a sofa talking to someone who wasn't ever going to be famous. Just when I was wondering if the punch had really been spiked, I remembered...

The reindeer were stoned. I had a vivid dream while awake, of reindeer eating mushrooms, the ones we'd been told were poisonous to average people, and wandering around, bumping into trees, goosing each other with their antlers, eating the mushrooms, and jumping into the air.

I was carrying a small pack with flint, fire stone, tinder mushrooms, and some dried meat, and I had a spear and throwing stick with me, but these reindeer were acting so silly, I didn't have the heart to kill one. The boy we'd traded a sister for said, "They get drunk eating the mushrooms. If you drink their piss, you'll see visions and can fly and talk to them."

"How do you get their piss?" asked Flat Nan, ever practical except when she was trying to get someone to sleep with her despite not having much in the way of breasts.

"Walk right up to them and ask," the boy said. He walked right up to one of the reindeer and blew it.

I had Ro for that. Ro looked back at me, obviously thinking the same thing. Neither of us wanted to eat the mushrooms or the yellow snow.

Al, who was always his alpha daddy's son, stabbed one of the reindeer and cut out the bladder and began chasing the girls and squirting the piss onto them, trying to get them to turn around and take it in the mouth. I walked over to one of the reindeer and asked it to piss in my lamp. Oddly enough it did. The piss tasted nasty, but I gulped it down and stood there. The reindeer looked at me. I looked at the reindeer.

And back in New York, I was telling someone, "Mushrooms, man, they will get you fucked up almost as good as acid."

"Mushrooms will make you sick," the girl said.

"Not if you filter them through reindeers," I said.

"And you're going to get reindeers where in New York?" she replied.

And after the drugs took hold, the reindeer and I started chatting, and I started telling someone the story, but in the old language, so he led me into a back bedroom and asked, "Do you have any friends here?"

"The girl in the swing," I managed to get out in English. "The chair swing."

He led me back out and put me at her feet. I kept telling the story as I saw it unfolding in my awake dream, but I don't remember if I managed to get the story all the way up to English, and I was careful to whisper so I didn't bother anyone. One girl started crying over in another time, um, place in the party, and someone pushed her out into the hall. These were a tough drug people, not as friendly as the reindeer. It was important not to bother anyone.

I put my arm on the reindeer's shoulder and said, "Why do you want to get stoned? I'm never going to do this again." Back in New York, I laughed.

The reindeer said, "Look, we're prey animals. We're too smart to forget that we're prey animals, but it's a pain to be always knowing that you're a prey animal and that everything from lions to dogs to you to eagles wants to kill and eat you and your children. So, since we can't dumbly forget like the horses who hang around you despite you eating one or two of them every so often, we pig out on mushrooms from time to time. So, kill me already."

"I can't kill you. I'm talking to you."

"That's the drug talking," the reindeer said.

I started crying and checked back with my body in New York to make sure I wasn't crying there. Nope, so back to the reindeer. "So what I'm imagining you saying is it's just the drug making me think what you're telling me isn't what you'd really be thinking?"

"I'm sorry," the reindeer said. "I'm just not used to sentences that twist and curl back on themselves like that."

"That's okay," I said. "What I meant to ask was isn't the drug giving me special insights, like magic, into your thinking?"

"Hey, man, don't try to make my trip your trip," the reindeer said. "I'm sure your elders and all those kids over there are going to have some magical explanation for all of this, but I'm a reindeer, and we don't do metaphysics. We just fly around after we eat mushrooms, and we giggle."

"You're saying just enjoy it?"

The reindeer sighed and tried to shrug my arm off his shoulder. I didn't shrug off. "Look at you. You've killed off the giant deer. You're killing off the mammoths. We're not doing real well, either, despite being able to sneak a whole lot better than mammoths. You'll probably eat us out of here. And you want to have me prep your drugs for you."

"But we love you. We eat you to assimilate your virtues."

"You know that most of what you people painted in your caves is extinct now."

This jolted me back to the loft party. I remembered the reindeer being stoned, but the acid was probably giving me a mental remix of what really happened. But then my life is often like that, first the ending, then the beginning, and then the parallel that happened earlier than the incident it was paralleling.

∞

Vel paused, holding an old stone oil lamp in his hands. He sniffed it as though something should have remained of the urine. "Nothing but dust now," he said to Carolyn. "Should I go into details about the sex or not?"

*"More just the blow-by-blow," Carolyn
said. "You can skip some of the details when you
describe your encounters."*

♋

I felt confused about what I was doing at this party and
remembered the first time I'd stepped into a Seeing. I'd
been around 16 or 17. What I'd seen was a bunch of guys
wearing towels and having sex. Looked like loincloths to
me, so I jumped right in, totally unable to speak any language in the scene, unaware that this was centuries in my
future, thinking it was somewhere else in the Paleolithic. I
laughed in the loft, thinking that I was probably now close
to the time into which I'd first jumped. I just thought they
had really better lamps somewhere else in the Paleolithic.
So, I turned to the hallucinating and hallucinated reindeer in that vivid half dream and said, "I remember you. I
haven't remembered you in thousands of years, but I must
have dreamed about you to remember this now."

The reindeer looked at me and said, "I'm long since
dead. My descendents are now working for the Sami in
Norway and dragging children around on sleds in upstate
New York."

I tried to fish though my memories for the real story,
the original drinking of reindeer piss. The reindeer said,
"You know you're not going to find all of it. You haven't
remembered all of it in so long those brain cells have
been recycled and recycled again. You remember better
the things you understood at the time, but only if they
were really different from day-to-day life. Big pains. But
big joys, too."

"That's not fair," I said. "What's the point in living a
very long time if you can't remember everything."

"Even I, who you're going to eat when you catch me next, don't remember everything. I suspect I won't remember anything of this conversation," the reindeer said. "Now will you shut up and let me enjoy my mushrooms."

"Sorry," I said. I turned my attention to the party and found someone really cute to go chase. We found the one bathroom that wasn't full of people doing lines of coke.

Under the light, he saw just how drugged I was and how young I looked. "You're balls- out tripping. I can't take advantage of you like this."

My frustration levels were about to pop my zipper. "I want you to take advantage of me," I said in the voice of the reindeer.

He said, "I'll blow you. Just don't follow me home like a puppy, okay." He wasn't the best of lovers, but I didn't need the best of lovers with my imagination burning acid. The reindeer stuck his nose against my asshole and licked my taint from asshole to balls, and I just exploded.

The guy looked at me and took a warm towel and began cleaning up, and the reindeer was giving me head and I came again. "Oh, to be young again and be able to endlessly come. I think that should be enough," the man said. "And other people need to use this bathroom."

I hopped up on the sink and waved my legs at him. "Come on, already," he said. He zipped up my jeans as I was starting to shrug myself out of them.

"Listen to him," the reindeer said from the scene inside my mind. "You'll be embarrassed later."

"I can give you a blow job you'll never forget," I said.

"My dear, I don't stick my cock in the mouths of people who are tripping their heads off."

Ouch, that hurt. I curled up like a snail, and the man pulled me off the counter and sat me down by the woman

in the swing chair, who was grinning wickedly at someone who'd come by to make sure she was okay.

Back in the half-imaginary, half-real past, the reindeer and I were sobering up. We hadn't been talking for a
couple of hours, just wandering about with my arm rest-
ing on his back, him being about waist high to me. He
rolled his eyes back at me as though he'd just realized he'd
been walking around with a human hanging on to him
for hours.

Most of the dogs had gone off once they realized we
weren't going to help them and we were acting as crazy
as the deer. One came back and sat down, looking eager.
My reindeer friend thrashed his rack against my hand
and took off running, the dog chasing him. I washed out
my lamp and pissed. A reindeer crept up, weirdly cring-
ing like a dog, and lapped up my piss. The other humans
looked wrecked. I supposed that I looked wrecked, too.

I got a cab home from the party, with two other people,
including the woman from the wicker swing chair, and
went back to the Chelsea, different room this time, and lay
down on the bed, not quite coming down yet, but aware, as
I had been aware 14,000 years ago, that what I'd done was
take a neurotoxin and semi-poison myself, and that if this
worked like alcohol, I couldn't step out of this time until I
was completely sober. But then I remembered I'd had two
glasses of white wine before all this started. And I had
wanted to follow home the guy who'd blown me, just like
a puppy, but knew that that was the acid, too.

We built a fire back by the reindeer the foreign boy
had killed and sat around eating it for a couple of days,
fucking, the way kids did when they made a kill off away
from the grown-ups. Flat Nan and one of the other girls
skived the deer hide, and we all stomped brains into it and

folded it. I wondered if eating a stoned deer would make us stoned again, so went off to find another one and killed a fawn of the season, so we had two deer and lots of time to hang around being young humans with each other until the girls got pregnant again from all the good eating. Better with mammoths because you could slide and slip on all that flesh as you were dressing it out, but two deer in the fall before it got cold and snowy and mammoth season were nice.

Hard to hide what Ro and I were up to; the het boys and girls were curious, and we were all just still stoned enough to talk and demonstrate. I don't know what the half-life of the mushroom drug is in reindeer flesh. The deer had bled out, and the liver and innards were foul from being left in the body after the foreign boy had cut the bladder out, so we probably weren't getting the most psychoactive parts.

"So, why don't you use females to put your cock in?" Ken asked.

Ro said, "Just don't. Females can't know what it's like to touch the pleasure thing inside."

"You have a pleasure thing inside your ass?"

"Probably you do, too," I said. "There's one you can feel up the asshole."

Ken looked like he didn't believe us at all. He asked Ann, "Put your finger up there and see what you feel."

Ro and I leaned into each other and watched while Ann put her finger up Ken's butt. She wiggled around and Ken breathed out, "Okay, but she can do this for me." Ann looked like she'd figured out a new way to wrap boys around her fingers.

The foreign boy said, "You can cut her a stick and make her a harness so she can fuck you."

"No," Ken said. Ann was busy cleaning her finger with leaves. She went down to a branch and cleaned it more. "Okay, so it's not just the one pushing his dick in who gets something from this."

"No, and we have hands," I said. "We trade off being the girl."

Ann looked at us as though we'd said something impossible. "What about this sucking thing?"

Ro said, "You should be able to do this just as well as we can, but you need to look at it carefully and find the little raised ridge behind the cock skin."

I said, "Helps to wash good."

The foreign boy said, "The guys who go for guy are good with their sister's children."

"We know that," Ken said. "That's why we like having a few in the group."

Ro and I looked at each other and smiled slightly. Ken was going to challenge his father's uncle sometime really soon now.

Flat Nan said, "Since I don't have good breasts, could you find me sexy?"

Ro looked at her. "Possibly, Nan. I don't think people should be frustrated. And women get smarter if they have children, I've heard."

I looked at Ro with some concern. "She's got a slit, not a dick."

"I could try pretending I was with you."

Nan started to cry. I wished I could give her tits or something so she could get laid without having to get my tenderhearted boyfriend to try to satisfy her.

First love. For all of us. Nan got someone to get her with child not long after that and grew a pair for nursing the child, so she wasn't Flat Nan anymore. I suspected it was Ro, since he was capable of being really generous, especially when he could use his dick to make someone smile. We didn't invent man-man sex, but I think he did invent penis puppetry.

The dogs got the hides away from us and ate them and the deer's guts and then ran home and hid in their own cave for a few days. Dogs hate drugs and scary things.

The grownups had taken a mammoth that refused to stop pestering the horses so nobody was really impressed with what was left of our two little reindeer. We all made some lamps and went hunting for tinder conk, those big fungus that grow on trees, so we could start getting things together for Bringing back the Sun, Winter Solstice.

I love Winter Solstice, still, having the family around. Never get tired of it.

Back in New York, I remembered all that, some of it again, some of it messed by the acid, which framed my understanding of what the first time was, even if the details were totally confused by what I knew about drugs in the late 1960s and early '70s. And I slept in and went running in Central Park, and we were still before AIDS but after Stonewall. I called one of the poets who'd told me we'd met (in that one's case, I had read enough about him so that I could fake it) and met him again for the first time at his reading at St. Marks Church.

But that's another story.

♋

We want to get back to the Paleolithic, at least some of us, and the last part of the Paleolithic wanted to get to our time. 30,000 years of chasing big game, less than that to get to atomic fission and high-speed computers. As long

as the ice doesn't come and scrape us off this island, we'll
be fine.

> *Carolyn remembered playing with some of
> the things in the storeroom when she was a child
> and being scolded when her mother finally caught
> her wearing a 13,000-year-old necklace made of
> amber carved into wolf heads, restrung every
> couple of centuries.*

> *Even the time-bound can't remember all the time.*

The Neolithic Shows Up with Sheep and Goats and Little People

We'd run out of mammoths. The ponies looked nervous. We'd lost a few of our people and some of the dogs to cave lions, big monsters larger than anything today. The temperature was getting hotter and hotter, red stags and roe deer showing up where before we'd had more horses. But the sea hadn't risen completely to cut off what became England from the rest of the world. The land between was just more wooded where the marshes hadn't started forming. Folks to the north of us were trying to herd deer. The mammoths weren't anywhere those days, during the first human energy crisis.

Little people showed up with sheep and goats and broad beans. They looked up at us and shrieked. They started stealing our girls, and they didn't give us girls in return. What became the North Sea was getting marshier and marshier. By this time, the family had decided I was magical because I could disappear and bring back food, but magic wasn't a big deal and magical people could bleed and die, too.

We'd kept our band healthy and at strength through my befriending people in various other times and bringing back food to eat. I took care of my family and myself. So, I was the obvious one to figure out what languages the little people spoke and learn them.

Nobody wanted to be a hunter-gatherer once the woods came up brushier than before. Then the water rose, and we were all stuck with each other on two big islands and some smaller ones. Our own girls that the little people stole came to steal other girls away, so I decided to go visit some of the girls who were now speaking the new language, the one that told goats, sheep, and broad beans what to do, and found myself attacked by dogs at the edge of what was the first wheat field in what became Somerset. They started plowing with oxen, which, like the men, were smaller than the aurochs that we'd hunted.

One of the girls came and told the little king that I was a giant magical creature. Through her, he told me to go away. This was his wheat field. I was wearing the wolf-head beads and had my hair braided in one plait down my back.

"But you've stolen some of my sisters."

The girl who'd been with my family said, "No, we like spinning wool better than spinning flax. And it's warmer and doesn't hold nits and lice when you boil it clean."

I thought that they could boil the nits and lice out of linen, but obviously, once furs had a load of parasites, getting them out was harder. "Okay, so can you teach your other sisters how this stuff works?"

Like everything, the new culture was controlled by yet another language, so we all began getting the children to learn the new language. I moved in with the sisters who found wool better to wear than furs, and learned the language myself. The king wanted to sacrifice me. But I of-

fered him my wolf-head beads if he would just fake it and
take over some of the land to the west.

We arranged the scene, and he struck me hard enough
to knock me down and ripped the beads off my neck and
winked at me. I stayed down while his people danced
around, then he took them off to one of their long huts
that they shared with cattle. I snuck off.

We kept them from killing our ponies until someone
came rowing in with horse gear and a language for telling the ponies to wear that and let us ride them and hitch
them to chariots. The ponies thought this was a better
deal than getting eaten, but we still ate one a year at Yule.
Everyone liked Yule. The little people added their own
customs to the ceremony, killing a man every so often.

When they buried the old king, I went into his grave
and got my beads back. The sinew had long since rotted,
so I put them on a braided flax string and went back to my
people with occasional trips to somewhere with electric
lights for chops and vegetables.

Then the Romans showed up, a couple of centuries after
we got the horse gear and the beakers. The beakers helped
with the beer drinking, and beer drinking helped with the
nerve to ride horses, but they liked pulling chariots better
than being ridden, and I was a bit too big for riding our
horses. One of the young boys built me a chariot for two
horses. I coated myself in blue, which was what everyone
was doing in those days, and drove off to see the Romans
who were coming in to steal horses. I felt we owed the
horses protection since they'd trusted us to protect them
against wolves even when we were still eating them if we
didn't make our meat quota with deer and boar.

The Romans weren't so tiny and were sympathetic, so
I learned Latin, which was not that different from some

of the other languages I'd learned when I'd time-jumped to go shopping. I had learned French and Spanish before I learned Latin. I traded the beads for a Syrian boy who looked vaguely like my sister, and got the beads back by trading tin ores for them when the Syrian boy turned old and died.

The family was living in Somerset where we'd been going to Bath for thousands of years, but now the Romans dug out and stonewalled the hot springs and started charging for the privilege, so people got very upset and joined whatever revolt was going on. I kept my family out of it since I knew the uprising would fail.

After we got apples and grapes, the Romans ran away. Some people who had been waiting for the English Channel to subside decided to cross anyway in boats. We found some people who smelled familiar—a branch of the family that had been on the other side of the water when it rose—and married them, while I began trying to keep the old little people and the newer not so little people from killing each other. One of the new people coshed me in the back of the head and stole the wolf-head beads, now strung on a fine gold chain one of the Romans had brought back from the east. This wasn't the first time I'd been hurt, but it was the first time I didn't know where the beads were.

And we were losing land then, too, as the newcomers stole our women for about three hundred years and sired children on them. I tried to keep our women together with the branch of the family that had been stranded on the other side of what we now call the North Sea.

So, we were growing apples and living in the area where we could go swimming in the winter in the ruins of the Roman baths in the hot springs we used to share with mammoths and horses and making cheese and storing it in the caves in Cheddar Gorge where we'd lived off and on since forever. And I couldn't find my beads, which made some of the superstitious old women wonder if I could protect the family against the various new farmers who were taking our women. The old women began to miss the small people and set out milk for the little people. And we traded scrumpy for a bit of being ignored and tried to figure out how to keep our land. If I'd had the amber beads, I could have bargained them for something. I found the beads again when someone else figured out how to get sparks out of one of them and was impressing the folks who came in with tales of dragons and gold. He only had the one bead, but someone else started showing the one that had a fly trapped in it, and I realized that if I hadn't been so distracted with the centuries of Anglo, Saxon, and Jutish invasions, I'd have just gone back to when I'd been coshed and followed the man who took them.

Or not, as I wasn't impervious to arrows.

The old women were complaining that I didn't have my magic without the beads, though, since I was getting nervous about trying to bring back food from the future. We were beginning to be conspicuously better off than a lot of the people around us, so I was trying to get the family to live closer to the lifestyle of the rest of the world. Getting the beads back wouldn't feed us, but it might make the old women grumble less. Or not. In a few years, the people I'd fed well after the Romans left would have died off.

I found the other beads by walking back along the time track from the two men who had them when I found them. I brought three of them back from the grave goods of the man who'd coshed me, then found the others in his son's hands and waited for him to die to get them back.

And the old women who remembered dressed meat from Saintbury's died. I went to what was almost China and bought silk cord to string the beads on from some of the family who'd been captured and sold east in Roman times. Silk wasn't as good as nylon for stringing beads, but it wasn't going to be so anachronistic. I found a little Buddha sculpture and traded it for furs in Finland, then came all the way home to find that the family had all turned Christian while I was gone. Some of them were sincere and fled the family when I showed up again to reclaim us for my magic. Others were happy to see me. I put the wolf-head beads in a safe place, moved my navel string, the dust of it, no doubt by now, in its little clay tablet, to a spot in the stone walls of the house that the family built, which was the basement of this house.

And we continued celebrating Yule with pony flesh and virgin fire, fresh for each New Year, as we'd done for thousands of years before.

And the beads didn't leave our land ever again.

Fourteen Thousand and Some Yules
[Thomas's Tale]

Vel's so-distant niece Carolyn came to visit during the week with a surgical kit. "I'd rather have a plastic surgeon do this, but I don't think that's practical. Thomas, can you help us? You must have had some first aid courses."

"What are you going to do?" I asked.

"Rebuild my finger tip," Vel said. "I want it healed by Yule."

"What do I have to do?" I asked.

"Wipe the sweat out of my face," Carolyn said. "And hand me forceps and scalpels. You don't have to do it fast."

And because Vel's immune system was so butch, we wouldn't have to worry about sterile conditions. I asked, "Why didn't it grow back already?"

"Someone burned it," Vel said. "So I wouldn't bleed." His voice was stiff, like the words were catching on his teeth. "I think if she puts in some cells from the other nail bed, I can grow a new fingertip and nail. There weren't any nail cells left, and the burning messed up the other cells."

I said, "It's going to look funny if it doesn't work."

Carolyn examined Vel's fingers as though they were a rock wall and she a climber.

Vel blew through his lips. We arranged his hands on trays with wax bottoms that Carolyn brought with her and taped down Vel's little fingers. Carolyn injected each fingertip with novocaine. We sat waiting for Vel to tell us when Carolyn could cut on him. He nodded. She poked his stumpy fingertip with a needle. He shrugged. She poked the other fingertip, and he flinched slightly, so more novocaine there, and a little more into the stump just to make sure. I rubbed his neck and felt how tense he was and wondered what memories this was bringing back.

Carolyn probed the tips of his little fingers again, and peeled back the end of the stub to wedge a bit of clean bone against the bone she'd exposed. Then she pulled the flesh up. I handed her the forceps. She took two wide stitches through that, with a gap between them, then cut the flesh on Vel's other little fingertip, then asked for a small saw, a whirring thing like a tiny circular saw, and cut out a wedge of that finger, down to the nail bed and beyond, through the nail.

I handed her the tiniest forceps, and she fitted that wedge of flesh, nail, nail bed, and bone and between the two stitches, then put in some of Vel's own skin that had been cut and pulled to an open mesh over all of that, and glued it down. She inserted some spongy padding where she'd removed the wedge of skin, flesh, nail, and all from the other little finger, and covered that with more of the surgical glue and Vel's own skin that she'd prepared earlier.

Vel huffed air out of his lungs, then took another breath and leaned forward to blow on his fingertips. Carolyn asked, "Starting to hurt yet?"

"No. They're just weird numb."

"I'm going put finger stalls over them both. Should take about two weeks to a month to see what we've done for you. I'll leave some painkillers. Thomas, you can take the fingerstalls off and check to see how things are going. Vel, if there's any sign of swelling—"

"—I'll be very surprised."

"Well, I'd hate to be surprised. When the glue wears off, let me know if I need to do anything more to keep the graft in place."

"When are you coming back home? I'll need help for Yule if this hasn't grown right by then," Vel asked.

"Thomas can help you get the Yule things together if you're not healed by then."

The finger the transplant wedge came out of healed first, digesting whatever padding Carolyn had put in and looking completely normal in two weeks. Vel pushed it against me, against a plate, and then against a lute string, fingering up and down the frets, grunting slightly, not playing anything. The other finger looked weird—not red, but lumpy, as though the flesh didn't know which direction to go, and it was still tender three weeks later. Vel couldn't finger his flute, and the gutta-percha finger cot didn't fit now. The nail came in, tiny and narrow at first, but the nail bed finally figured out what its relationship was with the rest of the fingertip. Vel trimmed away the end of the nail and wrapped the fingertip in wool and put a bigger finger splint over that. I felt odd watching him working on his left hand, but he knew himself better than I did.

We had cautious sex, which seemed to be particularly sweet for its slower pace. He ran the finger splint over me, teasing because I wouldn't grab it and risk hurting him.

Then one day in late November as we lay naked together, he said, "You must have a bespoke suit." I'd been thinking about buying us both leather jackets—he looked good in almost anything — but a bespoke suit wouldn't exactly fit my job.

"I'll wear yours if you wear mine." We went into London. On the train, I wondered how I'd feel about seeing him with his clients. He was in one of the stereotypical professions for gay men, an antique dealer, not that being with the police didn't have a certain fetish value that I'd fully exploited before I met Vel.

Vel asked, "What do you want to get for me?"

"For us. Matching leather flier jackets?"

He turned to me, one leg curling up toward the seat, a huge grin on his face. "Okay. That would go well with jeans. We could go dancing."

"Ah, I wasn't thinking of dancing," I said. I should get over worrying about doing things in public, like dancing with Vel in clubs.

"Okay. What's your objection to the suit?"

"I'd feel overdressed at work, and those cost a lot of money."

"Some tailors would make it look expensive. The one I'm taking you to will make you look better, and nobody will know quite why." He uncurled his leg and put it back on the carriage floor.

"We'll buy each other clothes for Christmas, then," I said.

"Not Christmas. Yule," he said.

Vel's tailor was in a small old building near the City. He looked anywhere between 35 and 50, was balding, wore wire-rimmed glasses, had an ethnic mix of assistants, but took my measurements himself. I said, "I work as a police investigator. I don't want this to be a suit that makes my officers think I've married for money."

The tailor looked at Vel. Vel tried to stiffen his face, then grinned. The tailor said, "You will look good in my suit. Navy blue wool, worsted." We went through the samples, Vel doing all sorts of textile conservator things like looking at the weave through a loupe, pushing threads around with a small steel probe. I picked something that looked like honest blue wool suit material.

We had lunch at Vel's shop, and I saw Vel in action with his rich clients. He wasn't obsequious in the least. Part of his charm was a slight bullying that I realized he couldn't have gotten away with if he were straight.

"You've been pulling shit like that for centuries," I said. "You're very good at telling them what they need to buy."

"For millennia," Vel said. "The only men allowed around the royal women and women acting like royal women who paid for accessories to prove it have been us or eunuchs. I'd rather have my balls. And the ladies run a bit of interference."

"What I do..."

"One of my sisters will probably tell you that I've always allied myself to the butchest man in my immediate vicinity, regardless of when. I'm going to wear your leather jacket."

I just loved him.

We were walking from the Underground stop to a shop that I'd bought a jacket from earlier, my first after I left my wife for men. I'd checked online and it was still there.

The shop was loud with music and various people running around talking about the clubs. Vel wore his bespoke suit, looking ironically both in and out of place here. He should have changed to jeans, I thought. The shop people ignored him until he found two matching jackets in both our sizes, black ones with shearling collars and oversized chrome zippers on the front and all the pockets. I tried mine on; he had gotten my size right, but then he'd been paying attention when the tailor measured me. I said, "It's a little too leather daddy, don't you think, with the zippers?"

Vel was trying his on, his suit jacket draped over one of the rack of jackets. "They match."

They were also £335 each, but I knew the suit he was buying for me was quite a bit more. "Fine."

"You wanna go to a club?"

"You'd need to change first."

"Tomorrow night, after we've been back for the fitting."

"They're not going to make that suit that quickly," I said.

"He's quick," Vel said. He handed me his leather jacket, put his suit jacket back on and began looking through racks of leather pants. He found something in black suede that he liked. "I'll take care of this if it fits."

I was looking forward to just doing something silly with Vel.

When I put on the basted-together suit still in the fitting state, I realized that my superintendent had always been dressed in bespoke suits. And that one of the investigators had been from time to time. I might want another one. The tailor marked where he would let things out and take things in. And we went back to Vel's antique shop and changed for clubbing. Vel cursed his shoes and the briefs he had to wear with modern clothes, then found sandals in some back cupboard, from Roman times for all I knew, and decided to wear those with socks and the leather pants without briefs and nothing under his jacket. I wore jeans and a tee-shirt.

We checked our jackets. I watched everyone's eyes, male and female, move over Vel's torso, all pectoral muscles and nipples with a nipple. Because of my job, I wasn't too much interested in piercings and flinched to see Vel with one, but otherwise, he looked magnificent, and I was proud to be his older bear. We danced for a while, then I let him go dancing with others. I liked watching him dance even if he was a bit clumsy in sandals and socks. Was he getting as much out of this as I was? He had the finger protection still on his left little finger, but stripped it off slowly, a miniature strip tease with teeth doing the undoing, and held it out for me to look at. While the top of the nail was still narrow, the base was now identical to the base of the nail on his right little finger. I kissed it and was happy that he would be a little less marked. We went back to rooms over Vel's shop at 3 a.m. and slept until my second fitting. As promised, the suit looked like a suit on me. I just looked better.

Vel made me feel young again. The suit made me look younger. The jackets made us look like kids from a distance.

The ring migrated out of Vel's nipple in two weeks. I found it in the sheets on our bed.

The Yule celebration was always on the longest night of the year. The solstice celebration had been old when Vel was a child, and Vel recreated what he remembered of the childhood ones, just with modern tools to build the limestone and soapstone lamps in the house cellar. He had a router that he was using on a few limestone blanks. Most of the older lamps were from a cache that dated back, but since Carolyn's wife, Maxine the anthropologist who wasn't in on the secret, would be here, he wanted to hide the very oldest ones, so he made twelve new ones to go with the ones that weren't so obviously ancient. He took off his goggles for a moment and put me to work making the juniper wicks, which was easy — roll juniper bark, lightly until the fibers began to soften and give, then with more pressure to round the wicks. We worked in the cellar under the stone house — and I realized the cellar, even with electric lights, was older than the house itself. Paintings on the wall showed animals that Vel had seen in Europe, creatures that never made it to England, like ibexes, and things that Vel had never seen, like woolly rhinos, 40,000 years back. I couldn't tell if the paintings were ancient or if Vel had just painted them a few weeks ago for me. Somewhere in between was most likely, since the cellar had to have been used too much for truly old paintings to have survived.

Vel looked up from his stone working and saw what I was looking at, "Some of them are from memory. I'd never forget what a mammoth looks like. Some of them are from memory of other people's art. The rhinos — we had no idea they'd been here." He pulled his goggles up and looked at the paintings for a while, not saying more, his fingers against his thighs, lightly moving as though they were remembering drawing these creatures many a time. Then he said, "I do more computer graphics these days, but the paintings were more sensual, tactile, the odor of melting horse fat in the lamps."

The Shetland pony he'd been fattening with maize was the next project, two days before Yule. The Exmoor stallion, wise to Vel's trick, tried to herd the Shetland back behind the mares and the gelding, but the Shetland came squealing up for corn. Vel put a halter on it and led it away with its nose still in the maize bucket. The Exmoor stallion buck-kicked the air then snaked his head down and moved the mares around in sheer frustration.

Vel took the Shetland toward the fenced yard where the yellow dogs lived in this age. He had a cart with ice chests waiting. The pony suddenly realized he wasn't with the other horses. Vel slit its throat with a steel blade, not a flint one, and stepped back as the pony's blood sprayed out and it collapsed. The dogs were all alert now, two slinking around. The oldest male wagged his tail low and licked his lips. He, like his ancestors, had been a witness to this many times.

We rolled the pony on its back and Vel cut the hooves off at the fetlocks and threw those to the dogs. Then he cut off the head, split the skull open, and pulled out the brains, putting them in an ice chest before throwing the two halves of horse head to the dogs who were swirling around the feet. The big male grabbed one half; a bitch the other. They began worrying flesh from the bones. Vel pulled off the hide and left the carcass on it while he paunched the belly and pulled out the visible fat. Then he tied off the bung hole, cut it free, and tied off the stomach and said, "Help me with this."

We were up to our arms in pony guts, liver, heart, and lungs, grappling them and lifting them to the dogs that snatched the mess from our hands and pulled the guts to long strands and red lumps. I said, "Isn't that wasteful? We could have eaten some of that."

"The dogs don't think it's wasted," Vel said.

He squatted down by the hide to separate more fat from the meat. I watched for a while. Vel looked up from his work and said, "You can cut the red meat off the bones after I take the fat off and cut it into joints. We'll add the marrow to what we burn, then split what we're not going to be roasting. We'll make jerky out of that. But leave the thighs for the spit. We'll hang them two days, then start them on Yule morning before we put out all fires and re-kindle them from the Yule log."

The dogs had buried what they hadn't stuffed in their bellies by the time we tipped the bones over the fence. They came up and took the bones away, digging when they thought we weren't looking.

"Don't tell the children we're eating pony," Vel said.

Vel put the meat up in a meat locker in the village and re-minded everyone that the house would be celebrating Yule as in the old times. He looked less and less like an antique dealer and more and more like a Paleolithic band chief.

Some family from London came; others came from other places in Somerset and Wales. We opened the great hall in the front of the house, which I hadn't seen since moving in with Vel. It was one large space with beams, almost as high in one great space as the whole two stories of the back of the house that we lived in, running long way sideways, it seemed, until I realized the hall was old-er than the two-story addition at its side. The walls were stone; the roof beams were newer than the stone. Some-time in the last 500 years, someone had fitted a chimney outside the north wall and opened up a fireplace inside the hall.

Children ran around with cut evergreens and holly, decorating. The young boys went out for the Yule tree, and the rest of us swept and washed the floors and walls and brought down from lofts bedding and cots for the floor of the hall where all the visitors would sleep while they were here. Except for the old ones—those would sleep in our room and Carolyn's or in hotels around Somerset.

Some of the bedding was leather stuffed with horse-hair, mammoth hair, or polyester. Other of it was silk or nylon filled with goose down or more polyester. Some of the children preferred several thicknesses of almost felted wool blankets, while some women brought cots and folding beds from the trunks of their cars, complete with sheets. We had around forty people staying with us—all family: children, straight couples, and more gay couples than in average families.

The straight women were easy with their sexuality, the straight men easy with theirs, and the gay men and women weren't edgy with the straight couples. The children were the family's children, no one adult obviously seeing to her own or his own. The whole gang of them had all the adults ready to steady them, split them apart if they squabbled.

Vel looked in at the family from the hall entrance and said, "In the day, we wouldn't have had this many together on an average Yule. This is a good Yule."

We went into the kitchen to see how things were going with the various small meats—and to check to make sure the fire plow and the stick Vel would use to start the Yule fire had dried sufficiently. Vel took a match and struck it, saying, "We'd have used this if we'd had them. We had pyrites when I was a boy, but the Yule fire we made with archaic tools."

Yule morning, Vel checked the shavings he'd use to nurse the embers, the kindling for the fire, the pony roasting in the kitchen, turning on the spit up in the chimney there, dripping fat into the flames.

He put on a tunic and wash pants, but went barefoot in the house, pulling on shoes and the leather jacket for outside. Carolyn arrived with Maxine, who fell in love with the house, seeing the levels of age in it and shrieking age estimates with delight. Vel began watching her, and she noticed and preened at Vel like a bi-girl. Carolyn and I shrugged our *Whatcha gonna do*'s at each other. Vel was wondering if he could trust her with his secret.

At noon, we all sat down for cold food the family had brought with them from their homes. All afternoon, people played music for each other, Vel playing something ancient on a bird bone flute. The children formed a crocodile and paraded around us waving streamers, banging on wooden blocks, and blowing whistles. I thought of all the thousands of years of this. Vel looked wonderful, glistening from sweat, his eyes glowing, teasing the children, grabbing the little ones and hugging them, then putting them down on their feet.

The winter light began slanting across the fields. Vel put out all the fires in the kitchen. He sat on the fire plow's receiving log, a log with a groove cut into it, fine sawdust at the end of the groove. One leg went alongside the fire log. The other was bent at the knee, bracing the log with his bare foot, toes spread against it. He bowed his head and worked the friction stick up and down the groove. As the sun went down, he had an ember, which he picked up out of the fire log groove surrounded by fine slivers of dry bark and wood. Cupping the ember in his two hands, he blew at it, cheeks puffed, eyes watching the children.

Carolyn and I filled the stone lamps with lumps of pony fat and put the wicks in them, then added warm liquid fat.

The children watched as Vel got a tiny flame going in the dry kindling he held in his hands. He quickly juggled the kindling ball as the fire in it grew, then put the flame in the hearth. After he nursed the baby flame into a small fire, he put a twig into the fire and lit one lamp. A girl of about 15 took the lamp in both hands, then she shifted it to her left hand and used another twig to pass flame to a lamp held by a boy about 13. Vel and the two older children helped the younger children get their lamps lit.

I'd seen this before as part of a Christian Christmas ceremony, but passing the lights had come before Christmas. The adults all sighed, including Vel. He then said, "Carry the lights to the rest while we get the Yule log burning."

Maxine, all anthropologist, said, "Fire plow? Isn't that Polynesian?"

Vel shoved the stick and grooved logs into the now brightly burning kitchen fire and smiled at her without speaking. Fire plows, being burned in the fires they started, left no traces in the archeological record. She watched the log and stick catch before smiling slightly.

One of the children said, "Can we turn on the real lights now, Uncle Vel?"

Vel laughed and said, "We need to show these lights in the windows before we turn on the electric lights and the real heat."

I had been wondering if the old stone hall was going to be chilly tonight, but it would be full of body heat. While the men scurried to set up boards on trestles and the women handed knives around, Vel and I carried the meat on platters into the hall. We ate the pony, partridges, hares, wild boar sausages one of the men had brought, wheat cakes, and frumenty that had been cooking for days into a burst wheat-berry jelly sweetened with honey. We had our own ale, our own mead, and apples, and we had created light to get us through the dark. Vel checked to make sure all the stone lamps were accounted for and kept one burning beside him.

After the children began to get sleepy, the adults moved them onto pallets, skin mattresses, and cots, along the walls of the great hall. We started getting visitors at the kitchen entrance, all the neighbors who knew when the house would be welcoming them. A couple of the younger adults stayed with the children in the great hall, while the rest of us moved back into the kitchen to watch a wedding dance. Vel relit some of the lamps and turned off the electric lights while two of the men pushed the table out of the way.

The man wore a breechclout. The woman wore a string skirt, strings dangling to her knees from a belt low on her hips. Vel blew bone flute music for them while they danced, him erect, her breasts glistening, four-thousand-year-old customs carried on by modern people too pasty-skinned to pull the dance off, I thought, until the whole magic of it caught me up in its graces. We all accepted that this was a dance between the two of them, that the eroticism wasn't to arouse us, but our watching was witness to their passion. And their passion was human because of the decorations, the string skirt and the breechclout, amber and malachite and ivory jewelry winking in the dim light. The woman's vulva showed when she split the strings with a finger, hips swaying.

Maxine was transfixed. Ancient ritual, modern anthropologist. Vel looked at me, then followed my eyes to Maxine. He raised his eyebrows. The couple went running up the stairs to the room that had been Vel's. We knew what they would be doing. Vel said to Maxine, "put on warm clothes and walk out with me. Thomas, you, too."

The voice of the band's leader. We followed him out into the cold night. He looked up at the sky, wobbling slightly. He'd been drinking. Maxine said, "I can see why Carolyn loves this family so much." I waited to find out what this was about.

Vel looked at Maxine and said, "Can you keep secrets? No matter how angry you might get at a person, could you keep secrets he'd given you?"

"Is this a secret about you?"

Vel didn't answer her question, but stood in the cold waiting for her to think his question through. Of course it was a secret about him. I thought he had to be half drunk to even consider telling her anything.

Maxine said, "This is a family with traditions. I think I'd like to know more about them, but I can't promise that I'll be with your sister forever."

Vel said, "Pity for Carolyn." I think he almost wanted to have a modern anthropological connection to his past, or at least someone with more than a lay knowledge of the issues and artifacts. I decided to listen as much as I could. He started back inside. We both followed him.

Near midnight, a young man stood guard over Carolyn and Maxine's bedroom while Vel disappeared. A woman told me I needed to go down to the cellar.

A masked figure naked with horns on his mask stood before drums that he was softly pounding. Vel, of course, but Vel transformed. Each of the paintings had a stone lamp under it. Hands moved me along to stand by the young girl who'd taken the first lamp. Vel took off the mask and knelt to us, "What I ask of you is that you protect the secrets of the house forever, and I will support you with my body and my blood as long as it is possible. Will you?"

And this is what Carolyn had sworn to him and what Maxine wasn't ever going to know. The girl said, "I swear that I will never be false to you or the family, whatever secrets you have."

"I swear that I will never reveal what I know," I said.

Vel said to the girl, "I've been alive since before these lands were an island."

The girl looked at the cave paintings, nodded, and then looked back at Vel. "I am honored, Uncle Vel. Others know? Can I talk to them?"

"The people down here know." Vel cut his hand cautiously and dripped blood on our hands. "My blood is on you. My life is in your hands."

The girl looked down at the blood and said, "You're not supernatural, are you?"

"I honestly don't know. I've just lived for a long time," Vel said. "I love my family."

"Uncle Vel, I promise." She raised Vel to his feet, and he kissed her on her forehead. She kissed him on each of his cheekbones. He came over to me. I kissed him on the mouth, smelling the liquor on it.

"Let's go outside," he said, fumbling his modern clothes back on with his hand seeping blood a bit.

We put on those leather jackets and walked out and sprawled down in the cold for a moment to look at the stars, head to head, feet in opposite directions, hands intertwined either side of our skulls. I wondered if Yules ever bored him. "Does this ever get boring?"

"No," he said.

"14,000 and some Yules."

"I've loved them all," Vel said, tightening his grip on my hands.

"It's cold. It's late."

"I could die doing something stupid like drowning in my own vomit while I was drunk."

"I'd roll you over."

"You won't be with me when I die."

"Someone will roll you over, Vel." I felt a bit annoyed that he was talking about his future death. I was going to be dead centuries before he would be.

"It bothers you?"

"Yeah."

"I wouldn't be talking about this if I weren't drunk. Sorry."

I tightened my grip on his hands, feeling his voice transmitted through his and my skull bones. "But you need to talk about it, don't you?" We were both drunk.

"I want to die doing something heroic. Does that sound stupid?"

"I want to die with enough morphine or heroin that I don't go out screaming in pain," I said. "And I'd like to die thinking you'll remember me some thousand years or whatever from now."

Vel tightened his fingers on mine, didn't say anything, but then turned my hands loose, got up, and helped me up. We, somewhat sobered in our drink from those words and the cold, went back in the great hall and settled down on a leather mattress stuffed with whatever hair it was stuffed with. Vel pulled a wool rug over us and we both fell asleep in our clothes.

But there was more. The children woke Vel up to see the dawn coming earlier than the dawn before this long night. We stumbled out and cheered the sun up, the children vibrating in my hangover, Vel utterly in his element.

Then we got our room back and stripped off the clothes and went to sleep until something like 2 p.m. I woke up when Vel, freshly showered, sat down on the bed beside me. "Are you ready to be awake?"

"Um, sure."

"Did you mean what you said last night? You really care that I'm going to stay young while you age?"

"I don't mind that. I like young guys. I want you to remember me. And I don't know if I believe it's possible."

"I promise I will remember you." He bent over me to kiss me on the forehead, stuck out his tongue and trailed it down to my mouth where he moved closer to kiss me again. I couldn't imagine that once one body had cooled, he hadn't found ways to move on to the next hot body, or he would have gone mad from accumulated grief. But I wanted him to remember me ten thousand years from now.

"Quarreling, We Walked to the Baltic"

The caves were old then, spooky places where boys went off to talk to each other and draw creatures we thought about on the walls — women, comparative penises, and beasts. And most of us were young. I was still bewildered by aging since I didn't do it, but hadn't grown new teeth yet. Everyone in my first band grew old and died, but I walked on with the children to what became France, and we found bands to trade boys and girls with. Still I hadn't realized that every band didn't have someone in it who didn't collapse into wrinkles and death. Accidents and quarrels between people killed enough before old age, so we didn't have large enough samples to know that not aging was rare. I didn't understand yet that my great-nieces were going to give birth and die for generations on end, and that I was going to live for thousands of years, and that the places I could step into were the future, not other places somewhere else. I had happened. I expected to meet more people like me.

So my band was somewhere with ibexes and limestone full of caves, speaking a language that gave us atlatls and darts and sprang and netting. The older women carved small samples of hair nets with their faces obscured and bodies as fat as dreams of now extinct mammoths could make them. Mammoths still lived to the east, we heard from men who came walking out of the cave-bear country.

In one cave, a dark man played a bone flute made from a crane's thighbone. He stood one foot against the drawing of a woman lying belly up and looked at me as though he'd been waiting for me for a long time. I suspect now that he came from what became India, not Africa; he wasn't that much darker than some of us. But he was tall and not round eyed — the women hadn't bred for round eyes and full beard as early as when he was conceived. He flickered, so quickly that anyone who wasn't me would have blamed flickers in the horse fat burning in the two lamps at his feet, or a draft coming from an unseen hole in the stone above us.

I moved to that second back to when he first flickered and back. He smiled and said, "I'm Yama, who doesn't die. You're the son of my sons."

"I was a child when my sister was a child. Now I'm with her children's children."

"I haven't found anyone like me before you."

I looked up-time and saw him dead, so he would die, but I couldn't tell him that anymore than I could warn anyone whose future narrowed to a wolf pack starving in the cold or a sudden rockfall minutes away. Time locked me sometimes when I wished least to be locked. "The short-lived ones will figure out that we don't wrinkle and fade after a while," I said. I knew I'd been born. "Were you born to the east?"

"I wasn't born. I've always existed."

I still believed in magic in those days, so I took him at his word, not thinking that perhaps he'd lived so long that he'd forgotten his childhood or that something had happened that had shattered it.

Whatever, I didn't know what he wanted from me, or if he still sired children on the bodies of his descendents, or if he lived off bats and blind cave things and lamp fat left behind when the boys finished their paintings and drawings and went back to sunlight and women to sire children who came back as boys and the occasional bold girl to add their visions to the limestone. Mammoth beads, ancient ones that girls in his youth made here ten thousand years earlier perhaps, were spread all over the cave country.

He said, "I even knew hairy near-men with long heads and powerful arms who could tear one of us apart, but who couldn't live to see their grandchildren, who ran from the spears and bows and turned into bones. They were here before we came in with language that wrapped around stone and set it in lances. But I heard them playing this when they covered their dead with flowers and ochre, on a flute like this one." He put the flute back in his mouth and played a song he'd learned from the Neanderthals.

I don't know now if I will live as long as he did, but I've seen more changes in the last two hundred years than he saw in twenty thousand. Still, he'd seen the woolly rhinos that I thought were imaginary beasts on the cave walls the first time I saw them and before I'd explored the future knowing what it was, full of reconstructions of the mammals of my childhood.

"Long time ago," he said.

"The time yet to come is long, too," I said.

He said, "It stops with me. You've come to help me stop time."

I wondered if he was right and all the dreams of flying metal things and lessons in ancient Greek somewhere full of cut stone buildings were illusions or another reality that I could step into as I'd stepped into the orgy in New Orleans when I was 17 thinking it was my time in a different place, with an especially strong foxfire to light the place.

He was the black hole of erotic attractions. I couldn't imagine sleeping with him. He scared me limp. But he fascinated me. I thought he could teach me how to live best as the kind of creature he and I appeared to be.

Now, I know that my ability to heal, to keep teeth in my head and bounce in my skin is something natural, just vanishing rare, and perhaps there's a way to explain moving through time other than as most things do, forward synched with the rest of the universe. But then I didn't know and he seemed to know. So I stopped there for a time, while my family band birthed and aged around me in a place where salmon and seals were common enough. He had lost his family band thousands of years before and left the cave to join us, dark man who made flutes and knew what stones made the best chimes and how to tune those.

The horses thinned, and we walked south into what he'd remembered as bison territory, but the bisons had all turned into painted creatures on cave walls. He stood in front of them, the rhinos, and the mammoths, and then walked with us as we turned north again, back to what became England, to carve cranes and something half an ibex half a stag into cave walls. I began to leave memory objects in caves that I recognized from earlier visits, things that would bring up memories tangled with them when I saw them again in the future.

He was more and less than a man, but I saw that he bled like a man when thorns snagged him. We walked back to

the place that had become sea some thousand years before us, where the family hunted the last mammoths and
followed bisons, now the dark ones, back east. I kept my
family band around me, and Yama told us where we were
going into this strange land where the ivory beads looked
different from the southern ivory beads I was used to. We
stopped to talk by a fire that burned for a few years while
I tended babies. Yama said, "So many things are gone."

I wondered how we could live without shedding seed,
except in my dreams of my first lover who I kept alive
until he withered and died in my arms and who lived on
as a ghost in my brain. But Yama was something too old to
touch, so I looked for a band who had a boy who wanted to
live as a woman. Yama found one and brought him to me,
a shy, shivering boy scared of being killed by wizards. Our
reputation as men who didn't age spread as fast as trade
beads. Yama took one of my sister's descendents for a season,
sired a child who vanished the moment he was born, who
we found dead of starvation on the ice minutes later when I
traced him through the umbilical cord, bouncing back and
forth from birth to death until he burned away his baby fat
and died. Yama stood with the tiny body in his hands and
said, "I don't want one of your girls again, ever."

The young boy, whose name I forget, said, "I have a
sister." And we fetched her, and the boy I loved and the
girl who slept with Yama both grew old and withered to
wrinkles. Yama's children had bad luck, died even if they
didn't panic and trap themselves for days on end jumping from birth to almost death and back before they knew
what was happening.

So, he turned to me, but the way he saw me was as a
man sees another man to subdue, not as a man who sees
pleasure in another man. I knew the difference and pulled

back from his hands that tried to arouse me. I've met more of his kind since, but not more with the depth of age, none that convinced me that even if he did bleed from thorns, he was at least part god.

I mistrusted what I'd seen, the future that went on beyond him, an illusion. The world ended with him, so we should keep him alive.

Yama had an excellent con going because he believed it himself. And because I wanted to make sense of what I was and he appeared to see me as his divine son, I listened to him, but he failed to arouse me for perhaps four generations of short-lived ones. The children grew up and died to ancient flute music. I kept my tally bones in a series of leather pouches and didn't jump into the future beyond him because he'd convinced me it wasn't real.

One night he doubled back on himself. Two Yamas grappled with me, held me down, and put obsidian to my throat, just holding the blade there. One of the young men of the band ran toward us, but froze. The gods were attacking each other. I knew I could jump but I'd leave my band at his mercy. He doubled again and said, "Why don't you double back and fight me?"

I didn't know I'd doubled, but another me showed up. "Because he believes you know what you're talking about, old man."

"The world ends with me."

"No, I'm from beyond your time. And I'm sure that time goes on after me." My double turned to me and said, "He's not exactly mad, but what he believes is the best he can do." I realized he was speaking to me in the language I spoke as a child.

I remember going back one afternoon while I was a curly haired barbarian boy in China and telling myself not to worry, but the damage wasn't physical and all the older selves in the world couldn't stop what was coming. And I couldn't stay with my younger self and teach him what he really needed to know to counter the ancient nonsense.

And I still felt the charm beyond the obsidian blade, and knew better what desperation the old lost man felt and how lonely I had felt realizing that everyone around me lived like flies.

Yama said, "I die? And the world goes on?"

My older self who'd seen him die and buried him and who'd gone on nodded. I realized then that what I couldn't see beyond was my own death. One of Yama's doubles vanished. I was left with an obsidian blade tracing a blood track down my chest. I didn't jump or move. I remembered what came next and went back to my Chinese patron, doubled even then, eating peaches that hadn't come to Europe yet.

I stared at where my double had vanished, then touched the stinging wound and said, "What do you want?"

"I want you to want me."

"Rape me if it would make you happy. I'll bleed and heal."

"I want you to die with me."

"Didn't happen."

"You've seen me die?"

"Yes, and I don't believe that what I see beyond you is an illusion, as strange as those futures are."

He sat down, and the first double vanished along with the obsidian blade. We both stared at the fire for a while. The band went out and brought back some hares and a small deer. We sat eating hare guts and looking at each other. The band went out and brought back a bison, and we got up and began moving. Yama didn't speak for days. He picked up his bone flute and played the Neanderthal tunes in different tempos. He said finally, "They died to bones. Ocher didn't save them."

I'd come back to the past and broken him. I knew that he was a man like me and that 20,000 or 30,000 years had given him nothing and that he didn't have anything more to give me than a wise short-lived person who would die, who would pain me in dying, but who could give more joy in an instant than I could find in Yama in centuries.

We both dropped our teeth then, the shift in hormones making us cranky as we grew new ones. Quarreling, we walked to the Baltic, picking up a few languages and women on the way. My young men shifted their allegiance to him for a generation, then living memory of the assault died, and I got control of the band again. My women gathered amber for me that I carved into wolf-head beads and gave to Yama because he had taught me some things.

He winced when he took them. I finally got the nerve to send my dick into his ancient body where Neanderthals had turned to music. I thought we were getting along well until I found he'd slit his throat on the day we spotted our first goat herders. He hadn't doubled to save himself; he hadn't reflectively jumped back from the obsidian blade, and he bled out having stuck himself as expertly as he'd stuck deer. I felt like I'd killed him by telling him he would die but the world would continue beyond him, as real as it ever was.

Then again, I thought as I took the wolf beads away from his body—the string cut and the beads scattered by his thrashing—he saw enough of the future coming to know he didn't want to be there. My band came around and looked at both of us, me restringing the amber beads, his body, and took the body off to burn in the new fashion.

And we walked back to Somerset before the sea closed. Our women ran off with the goat herders, and the boys shrank almost a foot and aged even quicker on wheat and goat milk. We had to get through the Neolithic, the Bronze Age, and then the Iron Age before things began to get better.

Flirting with Death and Old Men
[Thomas's Story]

Straight or gay, a time comes when no matter who's lying beside them in the bed, males think of change and a new challenge. Vel and I were being polite about our restlessness until one night, Vel raised his legs straight up, tenting the sheets, and said, "We need a change. Let's go to Amsterdam and fuck like whores."

Fat chance he'd remember me if we couldn't get through ten Yules without needing something on the side. I was going to grow old and he'd go through adolescence again, with new-grown teeth, according to his doctor sister, so many generations removed. Vel's body moved backwards against time periodically to stay nearly ageless.

But I had to admit that we were both feeling like we needed to be playing outside this special relationship, where we knew who we were and how it most likely would end. I would grow old and die. He wouldn't. A break outside the magical house in Somerset with the stone barns full of artifacts wouldn't be a bad idea. I could be a man with men like me; he could hide his magical self with a stranger. And Amsterdam would be an escape from being the proper-partnered officer of the law.

But on the way to Amsterdam, I wondered if he could love me when I was really old, what old flesh was like. What I'd be asking for might be a strange specialty for a boy house, but I'd find out soon enough.

I wanted to imagine me as Vel and an old man as me. Fuck my old age.

On the train, going through the Channel Tunnel, Vel read a book, shoes off, one leg curled under him, looking calm. I still loved him, but we did need a break from each other. He looked over the book, a thousand-year stare, and then looked at me. "I've ordered a ball-jointed doll of you."

A face that wouldn't age beyond forty, I thought, shuddering slightly. "Those dolls give me the creeps," I said.

"Well, I won't show it to you, then." I could imagine that he'd haul it out three hundred years from now and try to figure out which lover this doll face frozen in one expression represented, not the one connected to the wolf-head beads, not the one connected to the flint knife, not the queens in the vid, but Thomas, who'd only looked like this for a few years, whose real face moved and wrinkled and died.

I said, trying not to sound bitter, "Will the doll wear a little bespoke suit? And get issued a tiny gun from time to time?"

Vel said, "When we reach Amsterdam, I'll hire a cab for us."

I wondered if he would even show me the doll and if I could bear to look at it. Any of the ball-jointed dolls freaked me out. One that looked like me would be even more uncanny, a tiny me frozen in time.

The train pulled into Amsterdam's Central Station, a Gothic cathedral to 19th Century transportation. Vel knew where to get the cabs, and I, having few memories of an earlier visit, followed him. All I remembered was the train station from behind. I'd never been to Amsterdam without someone to guide me.

So, we took a cab to a boy house where the manager came up, knowing Vel from the past before I was part of Vel's life, which hadn't been that long ago for Vel. The manager looked at me. Vel flipped him a credit card and said, "Anything he wants except me," and went in the employee's entrance.

I must have looked stunned. The manager said, "So, sir, what would please you?"

"I guess this is odd. Someone old, seventy say, a top, still virile."

The manager nodded as though forty-five-year-old men came in all the time and asked for seventy-year-old sex workers. "One could be available. We'll have to call him in. If you'd like something while you wait...."

I wondered about Vel going in the door for employees. Oh, well, the lad had survived thousands of years. Sometimes, he must have done anything that got him what he needed, food, a warm fuck, and a bed for the night. "Oh, I'll have a drink. Gin martini."

The boys who'd been listening seemed to murmur among themselves and then focus on the next business-men who came in through the door. Vel wouldn't be out on the floor until I was with my partner.

I said, "How long have you known Vel?"

"Years. My uncle knew his father, very much the same sort of man." The manager caught himself before he said more.

We hadn't been at the bar fifteen minutes when an old man came in, looked at the manager who nodded at me.

The old man was gray and a bit shorter than most of the other Dutch, from a time before the present, maybe from a time when the Germans had invaded the Netherlands. Another time entirely. I nodded at him. He looked me up and down and said, "Younger lover, right."

I said, "Is that always the case?"

"Yep," he said. "You need me to be in charge?"

I grinned at him without admitting it in a word. He nodded back at the manager and took me by the hand, firmly, as though I was the rent boy.

We had a small but comfortable room with a sink, a jar of condoms, lubricant, and the house rules in Dutch, English, Russian, German, Spanish, Polish, Italian, and about four other languages with scripts that were non-European on the back of the door. Sex was to be with the condom, with enough lubricant that the condom wouldn't be likely to break, and with the house safe word, "past-tense," for any consensual activities that might need to be broken off.

The old man had taken his clothes off. He had a scar running across his belly from surgery or a knife fight and was slightly hairy. He said, "I know the rules. Take your clothes off and let me look at you."

I took my clothes off, careful with the suit, not so careful with the underwear. His cock rose to greet mine. He knew so much less than Vel, but what he knew was that his early childhood had been during the Nazi occupation. I wondered if he'd stolen to survive. He'd been a grown man when the German-era statutes against homosexuality had been repealed. He'd been an old man when prostitution was legalized.

"Don't just stand there," he said. "Grease your butt for me."

"Ah," I said.

"Don't tell me you didn't hire me to make you the boy."

"Yeah."

"You don't even want me to be considerate." His eyes looked into mine, then down at my very erect cock, and back to my eyes.

"You're right." I poured lube onto my hands and then worked it into my asshole.

He took my hand again and led me close to the bed, then took my neck and pushed me down to kneeling, then arranged me with my buttocks in the air and chest against the bed. He began fingering me, adding more lube, and rolled a condom on my cock, then I heard him open another plastic packet and roll one on his. He let me wait a few moments, then began slowly fingering me as he knelt between my legs, thumb pushing in, fingers working my balls. His other hand picked along my body in little pinches.

"Heh, Englishman."

I tried to say something but the words just fell apart. He moved in closer and opened me up with his cock, enjoying himself at my expense. I spread my legs more, and he shoved in and hammered me and grabbed my cock. I came, but he hadn't. He pulled out and said, "Ride me. Get me off."

I'd been here with Vel. It would be easier for me on top. I climbed over him and then lowered myself on his dick. He grunted and looked at me, then moved his hands to my own dick, not really ready for a new bout. "Now, get me off."

Okay, this was what it was like to be a rent boy, doing sex whether the boy's ready or not. I rocked my hips and ran my fingers down his chest while he grinned at me, his old man's erection not planning to do anything really soon.

He didn't touch me. I ran my fingernails around his nipple, squeezed his cock in my body. "What do you want?"

"What can you do? You're not even excited by this."

"I just came."

"Doesn't matter. You're trying to tell me that I'm supposed to get off with someone who can't have another erection for me, English boy."

Oh shit, why am I here, I thought, but I knew why I was here, and the old man knew what I really wanted. My cock was warming up again.

"You nasty boy. You really love this." He stopped rocking his hips and touched me.

"You."

"Yeah. You asked for this."

I was hard again and sweating. He said, "Make me come before you do."

"Let me..."

"...be on top. I don't think so, boy."

He didn't know everything but he knew some things. I squeezed and rocked and reached down to pinch my own dick, and he reached behind my fingers to touch the sensitive back of my dick head. And I came again and collapsed almost crying. He then put on a fresh condom and fucked me down my throat while I wrapped my hand around his cock base to keep him from choking me. He did finally come with his finger up my ass again.

He sat beside me on the bed cross-legged and said, "Didn't think the old man had it in him, did you?"

"I need to rest now."

"A bit," he said. "Boys are lazy these days."

"I really..."

"I could rest a bit now, too, but I don't come here for less than a day."

"Oh?"

"Another English man I've dated is here today. Has an older husband who works, has to slip off."

I wondered if he meant Vel. I didn't want Vel to be imagining me in my old age, with him. I said, "I don't want to have you go to someone else." I sounded stupid.

"How are you going to stop me? I'm here for the day."

"I can't possibly."

"That's okay. You can take a nap like a lazy boy, and I'll go to someone more vigorous."

"Don't say that to me."

"No, no, it's what you're paying for, saying that. You know it. Warm me up. Make me remember you out of all the tricks I've had since I was a boy myself."

That was too much, too close. We both stared at each other, unable to get back in the scene. He patted my belly, then moved his fingers through my public hair, avoiding the shriveled cock. I said, "I think we lost it."

"Well, let's just cuddle for a while and see what happens. So your boy's been a slut."

"He went in the employee's entrance when we got here, so I suppose he has a past I didn't know about."

"But you had a past, too, darling, I'm sure." He stretched out beside me and patted my belly just above the cock. I could sense that he was trying to consider where to go next, more humiliation, a bit of a pinch, asking me to talk about my own past. He rubbed and patted my belly while I just lay there and dozed off. When I woke up, he was jerking off over me, and I spread my arms and legs before I remembered he had a condom on. "Can't, against house rules," he said. He pulled my legs together and thigh fucked me. My cock flipped a bit but didn't rise.

"You really can't?"

I didn't know if this was in the scene he was trying to run or was a question to me as one man to another. "I don't think so."

"Oh, we can make a little bit of effort..."

He was running his fingers over my belly when the manager ran in and said, "It's Vel."

"What?"

"We've got to get him out of here. He's bleeding."

The old man and the manager exchanged glances, then I dressed, glad for once not to be full of jism, and followed the manager to another room where a medic was wrapping Vel's cuts in film bandages. Others were hustling who he'd been with away. "He should have used the safe word," the man said. "I wasn't trying to kill him."

People grabbed me before I could lash out. The manager flipped open his mobile to call an understanding doctor. Once the man who'd done this was gone, the arms holding me let me go slightly. Vel looked like he was in shock, but the house medics had stopped the bleeding. I didn't want to see what had been done. I shrugged the arms away and pulled out my own cell phone and called Carolyn in England so we could get Vel out of this before anyone figured out anything about him was odd.

The manager said, "I certainly didn't expect this."

"What was he trying to do?"

"Blade work. The man had wanted to scar him."

"Vel, or just anyone?"

The manager didn't say anything more. The doctor arrived with O pos and started giving Vel blood. I wondered if Vel's body could take it.

We ended up at a private clinic that sedated Vel, gave him painkillers, and glued up the slices. I sat in his room all night wondering what this was about, was this really what he craved sexually? When he woke up in the morning, I said, "Why?"

"He was paying a lot of money for it."

"And that's all? You're not kinked for that?"

"Not for the pain, no. I wanted to pass out from blood loss."

Oh, Vel, you bastard. You were flirting with dying. I didn't want to say that out loud, even if we had been alone. A nurse checked Vel's wound as we talked.

"Thomas."

"I called Carolyn. We'll take you home. We can talk later."

"You would have killed him?"

"I don't know what I would have done. People grabbed me."

Vel said, "I'm sorry."

"You didn't use the safe word, you stupid prick."

"I'm sorry. Are you going to leave me over this?"

I couldn't begin to think about that now. I just had to get him home because whatever was going to happen, he needed not to be some lab animal for the next couple of centuries, or blackmailed into whatever.

Carolyn came in and chartered a small plane to get us home, which probably took all of what Vel made from his scene and more. We didn't speak to him on the flight or on the ambulance ride home. He lay on a cot in the kitchen. Carolyn looked exhausted and grim, almost in tears. I said, finally, "You were flirting with death."

"I wasn't going to let it go all the way. The house wouldn't have let it go all the way."

Carolyn said, "And you knew if you didn't die, if someone stopped it, you wouldn't even be scarred. That's what's worse. It was just flirting with death for you."

"Thomas. Are you going to leave me over this?"

Carolyn said, "I wouldn't blame him if he did."

Vel said, "I've got the ball-jointed doll coming and everything."

I said, "I'm not going to leave you now," meaning that I would make some connections to time-bound men. We'd get careless. People would see me with another lover and tell Vel and I'd leave, the bad guy in the short-term story, and give the rest of my time to someone who didn't remember shitting himself over a mammoth charge. I'd leave him eventually to lead a small life with people whose lives I wouldn't share with a city's worth of dead lovers.

And someday, a thousand or two years from now, the ball-jointed doll would fall to pieces and out of memory.

He seemed relieved for now.

At a Time of Some Difference

Thomas left me. I don't remember anyone ever leaving me before, but as Thomas pointed out, perhaps I didn't consider some of the things that happened getting left, exactly, and perhaps I chose what I remembered out of 14,000 years. The little king with the dirty gold crown in the aftermath of the breakdown of the Roman Empire left me, but it's not like we had a relationship.

And I didn't and still don't understand what it is to know that the body decays and the mind shifts and loses the passions of its youth. I suspect I was never that kind of young anyway and I suspect an accident is the most likely way I'll die. Or murder.

So I make vids of the ice returning, of mammoths turning into Mercedes Unimogs and Mercedes Unimogs turning back into mammoths, the golden chestnut kind. And I make sure I know what the Gulf Stream is doing, and now I'm with you—young, understanding, cynical and sardonic in a way that Thomas wasn't. Who'd have thought Slovakia would have been so interesting and tolerant?

You're going now to where Thomas is dying because I can't face him alone. Yes, he asked me to come, and he knows you'll be with me. I promised him early on that I would be there for him when he was old and dying, and now he is.

So, we leave my new herd of reconstructed mammoths and fly to England. Graylag geese are flying overhead as they've done my entire life, none knowing they're born to die, each one another graylag goose after another. But taking care of mammoths, not hunting them, is a switch.

I don't know if I can manage the politics of here — I knew Western European politics since they'd grown up around me, Emil.

♋

Emil, a physician, looked at his companion and thought how odd it was to worry about surviving after surviving almost 15,000 years under far worse conditions than this. "Do you worry because you don't have much family here?"

Vel pulled his coat tighter around himself, and they got in the car together and drove to the airport. The man knew that eventually he'd be the old man in this relationship and that people would wonder what Vel saw in him. And they'd wonder about the young men who'd come with Vel to raise exotic animals, to recreate the aurochs killed here in the 14th or 15th Centuries, to breed mammoths from long dead DNA samples, along with saigas and the little dun-nosed horses with the eel stripe along the spine and the faint zebra markings on the legs.

They flew to England without saying much of anything. Emil was glad that Vel was willing to see his old partner. If Vel didn't weep for Thomas, Emil would be tempted to do as Thomas had done. He suspected that Vel had kinked to aging because all his men aged in instants before him. Vel never seemed to eye the very young boys quite the way he eyed the bears.

Or maybe this was just about Thomas?

That, too, was worth knowing.

"We're going to be there soon. Perhaps he has died already?"

Vel shook his head. Emil wasn't sure this was denial or just an understanding he had that Thomas would wait for him. With cancers, the end can be prolonged.

Vel was on his next passport, having not been able to get one by strictly family lies. He presented it at the customs line, nephew of himself since he'd had a string of British passports where he'd been son of some family woman married to himself. Emil knew that Vel's family had been bred over those thousands of years to be reliable. He suspected that he had some of that lineage himself because being with Vel seemed peculiarly right even though he understood that how Vel bred this into his family must have required some aggressive culling at times, though perhaps not for the last several thousand years. And even outside Family, people bowed to magicians.

Perhaps we are all Vel's family?

After they went through customs and found each other, Vel pulled out his mobile and called the kinswoman who was at the hospital with Thomas. He was still alive. Vel snapped the mobile shut. "Thomas is there."

Emil said, "The husband, right."

Vel said, "Yeah." Emil thought that Vel should have had more experience with rival other boyfriends after 14,000 years, but this was probably another thing Vel didn't tell stories about enough to envision them vividly. Vel always got his mammoth and always found his way home. They had a driver from the English family waiting for him. Emil wondered if he would go with Vel to the Yule Celebration after all this. Although Emil knew Vel had a Thomas in his past, he leaned back against the seat to listen to more of Vel's explanation of this.

So, he left me for a younger man who looked older. Whatever, everyone thought he was the bad guy except for the family, who knew about the brothel in Amsterdam. I don't know what I'd been doing. I told myself I was trying to earn as much money as possible for the move to somewhere that wouldn't be as affected by future ice as England.

I have a doll made to look like him—of him when he was in early middle age. I haven't looked at the doll in over fifteen years, not after I began to see why he was so bothered by it. The expression never changes, or it seems to and you know it hasn't because it can't but that you're looking at it differently. When I realized that wasn't like him, expression never changing, not aging, I quit looking at it. Does it bother you to hear me talk about him?

Emil said "No," but the story wasn't stopping for him.

The drive from London to Somerset takes so much less time than it did when I was walking back and forth across what's now the North Sea. I thought I'd take Thomas with me when I moved to a place that would be good for mammoth—somewhere with cheap farmland and warm enough not to face the ice again and high enough not to be flooded if the next big problem wasn't ice.

And he refused, but he came back when I was digging my birth cord or what molecules are left of it from the stone in the stairway. He was there to help me move, not to come back to me; too much had been said by then, by both of us and by the new lover Gregory, who never knew really what kind of man I was. Thomas stuck to his word on that.

I remember being drunk with Thomas on Yule, talking trash, lying on our backs in warm coats looking up at the stars.

I remember buying him a bespoke suit and how he was afraid that the other men on the force would mock him for it. You wouldn't mind another bespoke suit. I hadn't talked to you about Thomas because it didn't seem fair to you.

Emil shrugged. Thomas and he were the pet mayflies before the cold came back, before Big Winter hit again. This was one of the planet's hotter summers.

I'd wanted to take him to France to see the caves where I'd blown ochre against my hands to outline them against the walls there, where I'd begun to learn to draw and paint, being not really talented at art but having a long time to practice and improve. But we didn't get there. I'll take you, unless you don't want to. Everyone painted then the way everyone writes language now, just some were better than others.

And then I stood there with my bags packed, with a nylon case full of darts and a couple of atlatls, leaving to meet a ship with the first of the new mammoths on it. Thomas stood on the stairs below me, telling me he was staying with Gregory, that he was too old to move to a new country where he didn't speak the language.

I laughed. I didn't even know which language I might have learned that was an ancestor of what I'd have to re-learn. And wasn't I old?

We'd both made it impossible for either of us to change our minds. And I wanted one last fuck, me topping him hard. But we kept it civil, and he helped me move a couple of crates full of memory stones and some of the jewelry I'd made over the centuries for various men and got back from them when they died.

I sound harder than I felt at the time. My short-time man looked up at me with eyes I'd seen earlier on people at the end of the Neolithic, that decision that it was time to belong to an iron master.

I can remember him for centuries; I can't keep him alive. I couldn't make him come up the stairs with me before I left England.

♋

The driver in the front seat appeared to ignore all of what Vel was saying. Emil wondered if she was deaf, or if she'd heard the story many Yules ago. Did Vel's English family feel that he'd abandoned them after thousands of years of living their lives around him? Or was being dropped into ordinary English mortality a relief?

The driver, not deaf, made a phone call. "He's still with us."

Vel stopped talking as they approached the hospice. One of the women who visited Vel a Yule or two back and an old woman were sitting in the sun. They looked at Emil and at the driver. Vel got out of the car and said, "Does he know I'm coming?"

The old woman said, "I think he's curious about Emil." Emil flushed slightly and look at his shoes.

Vel said, "Is Thomas being awkward?"

The old woman shrugged. She said to Emil, "I'm Carolyn. You might have heard of me."

Emil realized she was in her nineties if she was the Carolyn who'd been the doctor. She looked ancient. Vel seemed to find it painful to look at her.

The driver asked, "Mom, how are you getting him in?"

"He's the nephew of a partner. And I've arranged it with Thomas."

Emil almost asked if Thomas looked awful, but decided not to say anything.

Vel said, "Is Gregory going to be there? And will he believe it?"

"Thomas wants to talk to Emil, too. Alone."

Vel's head bounced back slightly. Emil wondered what Thomas wanted from him. They walked in to the hospice slowly to allow Carolyn to move at her own pace, but her daughter didn't try to help her, and Emil decided that Carolyn would move on her own until she couldn't and then she'd die.

If Vel had aged, he'd have had everyone helping him. He had everyone helping him and he hadn't aged. Emil would have smiled at his thoughts, but didn't think Vel or Carolyn would have understood the expression.

Thomas was with a nurse and Gregory, who was on the verge of old age himself. Emil thought all this was going to be very awkward. The nurse said, "Thomas, it's your old partner Vel's son."

"Nephew," Carolyn said drily.

Thomas looked up and scanned the faces, then mumbled something and moved his hand for Vel to come closer. Vel put his ear close to Thomas's lips. Thomas bit him on the ear, nipped, not to draw blood, and said, quite aloud, "Liar."

Emil wondered what Thomas was capable of saying now that he was dying.

The nurse fluttered about and Carolyn said, "Could we be with him alone?"

"Yes, Thomas," Thomas said.

Gregory and the nurse didn't look happy about leaving the room. Thomas looked Emil up and down. "He's always had good taste in men. Now, Vel, you've seen me dying. You can both leave me with Emil for a few minutes."

Emil was acutely uncomfortable. Vel and Carolyn left the room.

"All my men," Thomas said. "He good with you?"

"Ah, how do you mean that? My English doesn't pick up the idioms sometime." Emil knew precisely how Thomas meant that and didn't know if he wanted to answer. Or if Thomas had the right to know."

"Is he delightful and considerate?"

"Yes, and a bit childish at times. For someone of his background."

Thomas sighed. "Remember he's human. Remember."

Emil waited for Thomas to add to the second "remember," but Thomas laughed a laugh charged with eroticism. Then Thomas said, "He came back. He keeps his promises. Are you planning to leave him?"

"No, not that I blame you for leaving him."

"No flirting with death."

Thomas appeared to be asleep for a while, but just as Emil thought he should get the nurse in, Thomas said, "Get them all out for breakfast, except for Carolyn."

"You're going to die then, aren't you?"

Thomas looked surprised. Emil said, "I'm a doctor. I've seen patients want privacy. Can anyone get Gregory to leave?"

"I hate competitive mourning."

"So tiring to have to comfort the healthy when you're not," Emil said.

Thomas sighed. "Send Gregory back in."

Emil went back to the waiting room and nodded at Gregory, who went back to Thomas. Vel said, "Well?"

"We compared notes." Emil thought he could safely smile now.

"Are you going to tell me anything more?"

"Yes. Thomas wants us to all go out for breakfast tomorrow, except for Carolyn, who can stay here. But we're supposed to take Gregory with us."

Carolyn nodded at her daughter. They waited to see if Gregory would come out, but he didn't, so they went to the hotel for the night. Carolyn had Gregory's cell phone number.

In the morning, Gregory was asleep in Thomas's room. They woke him up as quietly as they could. Emil noticed that Thomas sighed when they left. Carolyn stayed in the room.

Gregory said, "I shouldn't leave him."

"He asked me to take you out for breakfast."

"Yes, he told me to go with you. Carolyn is an old friend of Thomas's, but..."

"Too many men," Emil said. Thomas had strange tastes in men, perhaps. "He needs some rest, not to be thinking about desires on a bad prostate."

Gregory almost protested that, perhaps to say that there was nothing wrong with Thomas's prostate even though he was dying, but shut up. Emil ordered what he thought would be a suitable English breakfast, grilled tomatoes and eggs with toast and coffee. They'd just finished when Gregory's cell phone rang.

Emil knew before the wailing began that Carolyn called to tell Gregory that Thomas had died.

"I should have been there. I should have been there."

Not really, Emil thought but didn't say. He looked at Vel who was sitting like a stone, face like a doll's. "If you don't cry for him, I will wonder if you can really love anyone."

Vel collapsed into sobs as Carolyn's daughter helped move Gregory toward the car. "We can go later," Emil said. "This is Gregory's time."

He held Vel while Vel cried, not sure he understood all the reasons Vel was crying. The waitress hovered around them. Vel collected himself enough to pay the bill for the whole breakfast, then Emil said, "I suppose we'll need a cab."

Vel called Carolyn and asked if they could come back to the hospice. "She's sending a car when they think Thomas has had enough time. We're to wait here."

"Okay. Are you okay? I'm sorry for what I spoke."

"You shouldn't be. You don't mind?"

"I'll be glad if you can say you didn't do that crying in front of Thomas. He said he hated competitive mourning."

"What else did he tell you?"

"He said you had good taste in men."

"Cunt."

"And to never forget that you're human."

Fresh tears for that, not unexpected.

The car came, but not to take them back to the hospice. "Gregory is making ugly noises about how the family had a legend about it, of the man who never aged, the good Fairy, so I think you'd best be on your way," Carolyn's daughter said.

"I hardly got to see him," Vel said.

"You did see him," Emil said.

Centuries Ago and Very Fast
As Rationalism Dawned
with Some Religious Madness

I was scared of London in those days. But after Stonewall, I decided to visit the beginning of the changes. Now that we had begun a new Age of Reason I had to be more cautious about what I did. Between two or three thousand years ago and, say, 400 years ago, when threats got too serious, I could time jump. In superstitious times, my disappearance would be seen as just another supernatural occurrence. By 1726, the person who saw me disappear and talked about it might end up in a mad house. Or write up a very detailed description that would be more than "I fucked some smooth-skinned, slightly dark man with a little finger tip missing and a funny navel who made me feel very good about myself."

While I knew how the story ended in 1726, I didn't know how it felt to be in the story, and some of the details weren't clear from the historical record. But the full details never are recovered whole from my memories or the historical record. Complete recall leaches out, leaving stories behind. But the murderous people who'd cheered to see the molly boys hang and who stoned Mother Clapp almost to death had followed me into the present anyway.

I saw London just beyond the turn in the stairs, saw 1725 on a broadside, waited until the light changed, and walked out to night in an alleyway into November, on a Sunday. Nobody saw me, dressed in knee breeches and a work shirt and vest and coat, tailored in handspun after what I'd seen in museums of the clothes, a pistol under the coat with gold chains in my pockets and around my neck, stuff I could sell. Some coins should keep me alive until I found out how to sell the chains, coins worth more now than the chains were, then or now. If the Watch stopped me, I'd look like a thief. Coming to London then was foolhardy. But when I turned to look back at the staircase, I didn't see it, so I was in London with my own part in this time loop. So on to Field-lane in Holburn. In my vest pocket, I had directions to Mother Clapp's, the molly house, by the public house called The Bunch of Grapes and with an arch on the other side. In about a year, she'd disappear from records, believed dead, taken off the pillory in convulsions, headed for two years in a prison that killed at least as many as it released. And in the 19th Century, Field-lane would disappear under the Holburn Viaduct, the first flyover road to obliterate a slum neighborhood.

I knocked on the door. A little round-faced woman with a mobcap over light brown hair pulled back into a bun came to the door, with a man as tall as I was at her back. She wore a full skirt and a tidy shirtwaist. He was dressed in a wig and older suit clothes, embroidered and dirty. Beyond her, I heard fiddle music and boys and men singing. I said, "I need a room for the night, and I heard you were willing and a friend."

"Ye know anyone stays here?" She looked at my hair. The two of them pushed me out in the street and closed the door behind them.

"No, madam, I don't. I left the country in a hurry. Didn't think to get names."

"Do you know what people say my house is?"

"Friendly," I said. "I've come a long way, and I play fiddle when I need to."

She sucked on her bottom lip, then said, "Do you know what my house is?"

"For people like me, I've heard."

Someone else opened the door and came out behind her, a short little molly in full drag and a slight beard sprouting through the face paint and small-pox scars but fairer-skinned than the boy in New York. She wore a female wig. I smiled at him, her, whatever. "Sally, what do you think?" Mother Clapp said.

"What is he doing here?" the taller man said. "There have been entirely too many strange husbands of Mark Partridge running round." He was an older man, who looked about sixty, and was probably in his forties or early fifties, considering the hardness of the age, but he also looked stout and fit. I wondered if he was Gabriel Lawrence, who was going to be hanged, or Eccleston, who died in Newgate.

"Looking for a friendly place for the night," I said. "I'd like some warm fire to sit by, some company, bed." And said the word "bed" cautiously. Then said, "I can pay for it. Or I can fiddle for it if anyone would lend me a fiddle. Play pipes of various kinds, flute."

"That's not the issue here," Mother Clapp said.

"I wouldn't mind sharing a bed for the night," Sally said.

I said, "I can prove myself good for the bed."

They all looked at each other. I walked in between Mother Clapp and old Eccleston, introducing myself as Hal Turner. It's an alias I can answer to half-asleep. And everyone completely stopped talking and looked at me. Sally said, "We're going to have a wedding. Do you understand what a Molly wedding is?"

"I've been looking forward to things like this since I grew my first man hairs," I said, not bothering to explain how long ago that was. This was like an Amsterdam boy brothel a few centuries up-time, just illegal and a lot more dangerous, but proof of common brotherhood was always done in the same way. I was a little shy about doing it with the door to the bedroom open, but I had to prove I belonged here before I could get a bed to just sleep in, so off I went with Sally and found she wouldn't let me anywhere under those skirts, but my dick looked clean and passed a sniff test, so she blew me like a man experienced with such things. Neither of us got completely naked, which was sort of boring for me, but if everyone was a little nervous about being raided, keeping mostly dressed made sense.

One of the chains disappeared from my pocket. Sally had disappeared, too, no doubt with it, rather than wait for a coin. I got a room, just a room, and asked Mother Clapp where a man could sell a bit of jewelry if mollies like Sally left him any of it.

The jeweler had bought another necklace like mine a few hours earlier, I heard the next day. He gave me less for mine than I expected, but he was, after all, sure he was dealing in stolen goods. Pock-marked lad, short, about 24, had brought it in, yes. For the 18th Century, Sally was short, and I was really tall for a poor man.

The next day, I rented a room elsewhere and bought a trunk and strongbox with some of the other coins I'd brought with me. Forged a letter and assigned myself business in London from one of the family. Better not to stay in a room at Mother Clapp's after that, but I still went there Sunday afternoons for most of December.

The next time I saw Sally, he was wearing knee breeches and stockings and a very nice coat, weskit, and linen shirt, with a bought queue behind his real hair. I picked his pockets. The coins would be valuable up-time. Came time to settle up with Mother Clapp for the liquor, Sal didn't have what he thought he had and seemed genuinely alarmed. I wondered just how poor he was. He was about 5'4", short for men even then, except for the few city-bred men.

London killed almost three-quarters of its babies before their fifth year. Mother Clapp had prettier boys hanging around, but I'd read about two of them — Thomas Newton, who was old for a rent boy, rising 30, and Ned Courtney, an 18-year-old very bad boy indeed, both informers.

I covered Sally's drink with one of the coins I'd pulled out of her skirts. "Country boy," he said.

"City boy," I said. "You need another chain to pawn?"

"Whatever do you mean, sir," Mother Clapp said.

"Girl lifted a chain off me," I said, "but we're even if he wants a replay of the other night, but naked."

"Why?" Sally asked.

"More fun," I said. I pulled out another one of the coins I'd gotten from his pocket when I pushed by him while someone was copping a feel of the cock that normally hid behind women's skirts. I spun one coin around my fingers. While he watched that, I play-pulled a third coin out from by his ear. "Don't mess with a magic man, little girl."

Ordinary sleight-of-hand, that. He knew it, but he also realized where the coins came from. "You could have gotten those clothes out of me and had the coins extra if you'd been a very good boy."

I expected him to come at me with nails despite the difference in our sizes. I expected him to burst into tears. I didn't expect him to just sit there, stone-faced. The world hadn't been nice to him. He didn't expect the world ever would be nice to him; he wasn't going to ask the world quarter, either. He did get the suit of clothes from the theft, worth more than he could have expected to get. Being robbed by an apparent gentleman was just life.

Mother Clapp put her hands on our shoulders. "Please, not here. This is a fun place."

Sal said, "I'm sorry, Mother Clapp. I didn't know he was a fucking pickpocket as well as a thief."

"I didn't steal the chain," I said.

"Well, sorry. Now I've got to whore something up for dinner and bed, and I obviously have no brains at all in picking who to gull."

He'd have been a presentable boy without the pockmarks, and by the standards of the times, he wasn't badly scarred. "Can we try this again, with the door closed this time?"

"No, fuck off."

He started making a play for someone who just felt iffy to me, and I wondered if he'd end up with the worst pox, or if he had another male name that was on the Old Bailey records. I shrugged and looked back at Mother Clapp who said, "He came up a poorhouse baby."

Ninety percent of those didn't make their fifth year.

I said, "I wish he hadn't lifted my chain. T'was what I had to get by until I find a way to make my way in London."

I had family in the city, but wasn't sure the conditions of the time loop would let me approach them. We'd just built a store with rooms over it in a respectable part of town. Two family women, a paired couple, took care of the store, putting Hogarths and good first edition books away for the future. I knew the address since I'd picked the place for the store. It would stay a reasonable neighborhood for an antique store from 1715 to 2007, and probably on.

"I bet he wishes he hadn't lifted it either," Mother Clapp said. "Why don't you give him at least one of the coins back so he doesn't have to go off with that scurvy Mark Partridge."

Fuck. Partridge was an informant because he was pissed-off when his lover outed him, Neither all that faithful or sane, Partridge was informing for the Society for the Reformation of Manners, who called the regular police to do their duties and bust these people and hang them. Partridge was pretty, but sullen and nervous. While some people were willing to let him blame Harrington for gossiping too loud, others weren't. People here were being polite to him, but nobody was going near him, even without any of his special new husbands by his side.

I went up and said to Partridge, "Leave him alone, Mark." I handed all the coins back to Sal, who shuddered and took them, and walked out of the building into the street. He had other places he could go now, to get away from my condescension and Partridge's creepiness. I couldn't reveal what Partridge and his friends were going to do—the paradox loop decided this wasn't something I ever could speak aloud to these people—so there. I also suspected that if I could warn them, everyone in the house would suspect me of being yet another informer, but Mother Clapp seemed nervous enough about Partridge.

The old master of ceremonies, Eccleston, called me over. "He's not a purely bad boy, but you looked like a coney, ye'know. Country man all guileless, even if a gentleman."

I shrugged. By this time, one of the fiddlers was tired-armed, so I got tapped to play and rosined up the bow and played dance music for those dead men.

Sal came back in and hunkered down at my feet. I guess everyone in the past who caught him stealing either beat the crap out of him or took it out on his ass whether he liked it or not. I reached down between dances and ruffled his hair. He ducked his head but stayed squatting where he was. "It's cold out."

"Thought you'd be off to The Royal Oak or Mr. Wright's."

"Thanks for pulling me away from Partridge. She's a bitch. Sorry I fucked with you, but don't you really like the clothes on me?"

"Honest, those clothes are worth twenty times one blow job."

"Well, not what I could get for them if I pawned them," Sal said, hauling himself to his feet. "How did you do that thing with the coin out from behind my ear?"

I wondered if I was the kindest and least threatening man in the room tonight, or whether Sal was going to see what else I had in my drawers. "What were you called before you became Sally?"

"Thomas Phillips. I live here, been living here almost two years."

The one who disappeared after the raids, I thought with some relief. "So you had a bed, regardless?" And good for me not to be living here.

"I can't keep owing Mother C, you know."

I didn't tell him that I thought he could. "She's fond of us all. We're her fabulous friends."

"Full bare body is going to cost you," Sally said.

"I'm good for it," I said. "I had another necklace I sold same place you sold yours."

"If they're not stolen and you can warrant that, there are better places to sell jewelry," Sal said. "I could have taken the both of them. You took all my money."

I shrugged. We called Eccleston over and Sal said he'd take me up to his room, but he was going to get his clothes back. Eccleston looked at me and said, "I'd like to keep hold of your sidearm, sir."

Okay, fine. Sal said, "We'll need a fire laid in, don't you think."

I wondered if I could get some hot water added to that. "And a kettle of wash water. And a candle."

Sal said, "Oo, he's fancy."

We stood around rather shyly while Mother Clapp went up to the rooms to set a fire. I wondered how cold it was on the upper floors. Her dancing room was warm, but that was probably as much the bodies crowded in it as the coal fire in the grate. Eccleston kept his eyes on me. "Yer not to take his clothes," he said.

Everyone was watching us. Nobody quite knew what to make of me with my poor clothes, natural hair, and expensive pistol. I realized my accent was identifiably country posh, if anyone knew Bath at all.

All that attention was exciting. Mother Clapp came down and charged me 10 pence for the fire, tu'pence for the candle, and said she'd have to think about how much a bucket of warm wash water would cost me. I followed Sal up the stairs. The room was dim, even for afternoon in 18th-Century London. I stuck a sliver of wood in the coal fire and brought out a flame to light the candle. Then I began peeling my clothes off first. Sal had his eyes fixed on my cock. "I expect my gentlemen to be more excited than that." I began stripping him, wondering what kind of lice I was going to get from this, and then unfastened his little queue and gave him a kiss before taking a look at him with candlelight. He was a bit bowlegged from rickets, and quite thin and very pale. The room was cold. I took a closer look at his cock, let it bounce on my palm, and lit his skin inch by inch with the candle about six inches from him, holding his upper right arm. The cock looked okay. I turned him around, and he looked as healthy as I could expect an 18th-Century boy whore to look.

"I'm cold," he said.

"Let's get in the bed now," I said. He arranged himself on his knees, ass up, but I found we had two blankets on the bed, plus my greatcoat. I brought the greatcoat over to the bed and pulled out the lube that I'd brought packed in a period flask and slathered it around. If I were caught with my cock up a boy's butt by the laws, anachronistic lube was going to be the least of my worries, and I knew this stuff was hypoallergenic. Sal looked cute and tiny with my greatcoat covering his shoulders, and I lay down in the bed, my fist putting lube on my cock, and pulled him around and over, facing me, on my dick, the coat still covering his shoulders and the tops of my thighs, his front naked for touching from face to dick.

Genuinely turned on now, he began moving up and down. I pushed against him and touched his lips with my fingers, then tapped down his body, running my fingers in circles around his nipples. I gave him my ungreasy hand and he leaned back and his dick was floating over my belly. He was throbbing down in his bowels. I reached up and stroked the underside of his dick with my still slippery hand and he shrieked and came all over my belly. I came watching him spurt.

And Eccleston heard the shriek and shoved the door in, my pistol in his hand, and a bunch of other mollies came pounding up the stairs. I threw my hands in front of my face. Sal said, "No, it's okay. Really."

I was still inside Sally. Everyone gathered around the bed with huge grins on their faces. "Sal on top?" someone in the back asked, sounding totally amazed.

Eccleston put the pistol in his belt and whipped away the greatcoat, which Sal had pulled around us when the men came running up. He said, "Country boy has his dick up Sally, but Sally has come all over country boy's belly. Welcome to London, country boy. This is what they hang you for."

Mother Nell came pushing through the boys holding candles and rush lights. She was holding the pail of warm water. "I guess it's time for this. Did he come inside Sal?"

I was blushing and getting another erection inside Sal who made a little gasp before he leaned over to bite my nipples. I tried to hold myself still, but Eccleston said, "It's bad for a man not to go when he needs to go. And we want to see what you did with Sal. Show us, country boy."

"Pop Sal off and let someone else ride," a voice from the crowd said.

"No," I managed to say. Mother Clapp got most of the crowd to back out.

One of the men who stayed came up to the bed and kissed and tongued my flanks. I didn't reach up for Sal's cock this time. After I'd finished, Sal gravely bent down to kiss me on the mouth and pulled himself off me. Eccleston sat down on the edge of the bed and stroked my hair while Sal cleaned himself off with the wash water and some towels. He said, after my breathing returned to normal, "You been a good sport. You're a handsome man." His finger circled around and in my navel as if memorizing how it wasn't like other navels, then he cleaned Sal's sperm off my belly while I held my arms over my head.

I wanted to take a nap right then. Sal and Eccleston lay down in the bed with me, probably their bed, and we went to sleep until dark, nothing more happening. I wondered what Sal was to Eccleston and what happened to him when he absconded. And then wondered if Eccleston died after hearing that Thomas Newton turned informer rather than hang, if you could hear things like that in prison.

And by now it was December, and I was feeling lonely in my rented room and spent a fair amount of time at Mother Clapp's, without Mark Partridge showing up again, with me mostly fiddling. I went by the shop my family kept and felt awkward about being a double in this time, remembering the names of the women, Isabel and Rose, both family, both knowing what I was and could do, as far as anyone in the 18th Century could understand it. I needed better clothes and a wig if I was to visit them, not this workingman's used clothes of a fop rig that I'd bought with Sal's help.

One of them saw me watching the shop and came out cautious. "Are you the real he or a double?"

"Double," I said.

"Why?"

"In house time, I was careful to stay away from London, to keep to family and places good for me. I just wanted to see what it was like now that I know what the history is."

"From the future," she said. "Figures. You've had some things dropped off by another double. I'm supposed to tell you it's louse wash and something for the bloody flux and gonno-something." She handed me a cloth bag heavy with a couple of bottles of crab and louse shampoo, repackaged in blown-glass flasks, and a couple of smaller bottles filled with two different kind of pills.

I wondered what had happened and for whom I'd need antibiotics. I took the packages and left them in my room in the trunk, then went back to Mother Clapp's.

Sal had the bloody flux from the city water or off food and since my bout with him had picked up a raging case of gonorrhea. The future double had guessed protozoan but had included some other antibiotics, which would take care of that. I fed Sal all the anachronisms and realized I couldn't just get him over this. I had to get him well beyond simply not bleeding out of his ass and not having gonorrhea. I had to get him to leave Mother Clapp's.

Isabel and Rose invited me to lunch at the shop. I was reluctant to go, but the other time double had given me more than one bottle of the crab shampoo, so I bought new clothes and a wig. After I shaved my head, I put the wig on and went to lunch with my family folk.

"So, what was that about?" Isabel, who'd been the one who'd handed me the package said. I remembered which one was which when I thought more about Christmas the next year.

"Molly houses."

"You picked someone up who you want to try to help? And even here we know that some idiot was ranting about some other idiot telling people he was a molly, had an inclination toward his own sex. Do we need this?"

"I'm going to get him out of London for a while. Can you think of anything?"

"We're going to Yule at the family house," Rose said. She was the blonde, or was wearing a blonde wig. "When we're back, let's have lunch with him, at your rooms. If he's salvageable, if he could help the family...what are we saving him from, by the way? Besides getting poxed."

"Hanging for sodomy or getting his friends hanged for sodomy. But he does disappear, so I think we've got a chance."

"Or he just disappears on his own," Isobel said.

"He's off the game now," I said. "Colon is still raw. I'll have to help him out some."

My family is unflappable these days, but I wasn't sure the 18th Century time-bound would be unperturbed about helping a rent-boy escape the gallows just because a double from the future wanted to do this. Isobel almost tried to say something, but stopped short.

I took Sal, also known as Thomas Phillips, to my rooms as soon as he stopped shitting but while he was still weak. One of the other mollies sold oranges, so I fed Sal oranges and the freshest pilchards I could buy in London, and good wheat bread, and sprouted cress for him, and then found peas that would sprout and fed him those over his protests that he wasn't a rabbit. He went with me when I looked for old needlework and knew some places where I could find more of it than I'd known about in the day. He loved rummaging through old clothes, and had an eye for things that were hopelessly outdated for 1726, but which were still made well and would be museum pieces in the 20th Century. We weren't fucking because he was still healing from the flux and wasn't sure he didn't have gonorrhea still. I took him to Brighton for most of January, to a cold beach and a warm cottage that was for let cheap, and kept feeding him and getting him to walk more. He gained weight and didn't look so fragile, which might have cost him in the bedroom but which made him look like he could survive better the next time he was fluxed or clapped. I liked having a body in bed with me, sleeping. Bodies sharing my bed made me feel safe.

Sal missed London, so we came back around 23 January 1726. And on Sunday, I took him to my rooms for lunch with my kinswomen, who came dressed as men. In a second, Sal made them as cross-dressing women. They pulled off their male wigs and sat down to dinner in skullcaps. Isobel asked Sal, "Where were you born?"

Sal said, "Workhouse somewhere." They encouraged him to say more. With the help of some fine ale and roast beef from the cook shop three doors from my rooms, he began talking. I hadn't heard him talk so much in nearly three months of knowing him. He was talking to earn our trust, to see if we condemned him utterly for what he'd been, and he was funny and vulnerable. While what he'd said would have hanged him several times over, none of it involved being treacherous to his friends or much of a thief. Then he realized that he'd been talking rather much and said, "Sorry."

Isobel asked, "What would you want to do with your life if you could change it?"

"I'd go to America and sell clothes. Philadelphia. They don't hang people for sodomy there, just whip them and take a third of their property. And they haven't bothered to do much of that, I hear. They've got a bachelors' club."

Rose said, "That might not mean what you think it means. What kind of clothes?"

"Used ones. I'm not a tailor, yet."

"And can you read and write?" I asked.

"I can do some ciphering and a bit o' writing."

"Can you wait outside?"

He went outside. I shut the door and said, "So, what do you think?"

Rose said, "He stays, he hangs or gets his friends hanged, if they take him. If he goes to Philadelphia now, he's got some chance of doing better than being an aging boy whore."

"Or he dies in transit," Isobel said.

"Then it's the same as if he got hanged, only he isn't tempted to shit on his friends," I said.

Isobel asked, "Do you trust him enough to front him clothes?"

I said, "No, but I'd risk three trunks of used clothes just to give him some hope."

Rose said, "Two. And we'll tell him where to send the remittance and see what happens."

I didn't really want to put the shop at hazard, but nothing bad had happened yet. "And I've got to tell you to invest in the anonymous *Gulliver's Travels* book when that's printed. It's really by Jonathan Swift. Also, buy Hogarths."

"Hogarths are dear now. Now can you go back to your home time?" Isobel asked.

"I don't feel I can," I said, "so there's more."

When I went back outside, I didn't see Sal at first, but then saw him hunkered down by the door, face bleak and eyes looking like he'd expected to be shown the door and asked to wait forever outside any place decent. Isobel came out and took his hand and led him back inside and said, "We'll front you two trunks of clothes and pay your passage so you don't have to go in steerage. We want to do business with you."

We got Sal all packed up and ready to leave by January 31. He spent some time at Mother Clapp's, whoring together a bit more for the trip. I was sure he'd abscond, just not sure that he'd end up on that Philadelphia boat. At the next to the last minute, he didn't want to leave his friends. I took Eccleston aside and asked him if heading to Philadelphia would be a good move for Sal.

"He's talked about going as an indenture for years, but that's a nasty way to travel, like in a prison. He's just got over the bleeding flux and I thought he was clapped, but he doesn't appear to be. If he stays here, I don't know."

"My family can help him."

"Always figured you for a toff. Not a bad toff, though. Game." The old man looked at me wistfully, as though he knew this wasn't for him and couldn't be. No reason to see his mate not get the prize.

"Who has Sal been with beside me?"

"About everyone who's sensible. He's a nicer boy than most, if you look beyond what the small pox did to his face."

"He stole from me the first day I was here."

"You know how many toffs show up and make a mess out of someone?"

I shrugged. "So, can you suggest what it would take to get him to get on the ship next week."

"Yeah, I'll talk to him." He stopped and looked at me. "Can you show me that trick with the greasy hand stripping the come out of a cock?

"Oh, sure," I said.

We all saw Thomas Phillips walk up the gangplank to the ship — my ladies of the family, myself, Mother Clapp, and Eccleston and William Griffin, who'd been sure up to then that I'd been an informer — and waved kisses to him and danced back and forth on the pier. And the ship floated down the Thames from the docks with tea and clothes and pottery, and a couple of passengers amongst the sailors. Whatever happened to him, he got to miss the raid the next week.

My family members got in a hackney back to the better part of London, and I went back to Mother Clapp's with the other mollies. Eccleston and I sat in the afternoon, drinking tea that I'd bought him for a treat. He said, "I'd like you to show me that greasy hand trick."

"I've never figured you for the woman role," I said.

"I was a right smart maiden in the day," he said. "Even being tall."

"Oh?"

"But I've been hung up with something in me."

"Prostate?" I said, not sure he'd know what that was.

"Yeah, but I'd have to adjust my thinking if I was to put it to you. And I'm poxed. I wouldn't want to pass that on."

I always carry lube. "I can drape myself in silk if that would help. And I don't catch the pox. It's been tried before. I just don't catch it."

"Well, then, let's try that on top thing."

I thought of him dying in prison, and didn't know if this was a good idea or not, getting too attached to a man who would die badly. But then, if he was going to die in prison, betrayed by Thomas Newton and Mark Partridge, the old man deserved a bang before that. "I'd be honored, Mr. Eccleston."

He grinned, showing broken teeth. I brought my face up close to his. Instead of kissing him mouth to mouth, I rubbed my nose against his. Then kissed him, feeling the broken teeth with my tongue. He kissed me back. We wrestled with our tongues for a while, and then broke off laughing.

Mother Clapp watched the door for us while we went in to the double-bedded room on the ground floor. Under the covers, I went up and down Eccleston's body with my tongue, then decided I could be cold this once for the sake of him getting an eyeful. As I lubed him and me, his eyes widened at the different feel of it — not grease at all. Then I put myself slowly on his cock and asked for his hands and leaned back, and we moved in slow spirals for a while. He felt my cock floating over his belly but didn't go for the underside of it. I saw some ancient mischief in his eyes and closed my eyes so I could be surprised. His fingertips made slight circles on my eyelids, and then he trailed his nails down my body. I rocked to get pressure against my prostate and cock root, then he began teasing the underside of my cock with his fingers, while moving his hips up and down as much as he could with me on top of him. I squeezed a bit, and he groaned, but kept firm inside me. He's an old man, I thought, he could take a while. He was keeping me hard, pulling back from setting me off. I opened my eyes and saw him smiling up at me. "It's a beautiful sight, a young man riding my cock, sweating." He took his hands away from my cock and ran his fingers, nail side against my skin, from my nipples back to my cock. One hand went to grip the base of my cock, the other played along the bottom of it, and I spurted on his belly. He still didn't come, but pulled out and flipped me over and put me on my knees and rammed me from behind, finally being able to think of me that way, I supposed. We collapsed, rolled belly to belly and kissed lightly. "Now, they can hang me," he said. I flinched, but his eyes were closed.

Hanging was nasty before the drop. People could take up to a half hour to die. The execution crew got the prisoners drunk between Newgate and Tyburn so their bladders releasing said they were dead. When urine ran down the hanged man's legs, the crowd would go silent.

I stayed on playing fiddle until the raid. I couldn't save them all, but I could be a witness. The Sunday, they came, everyone stopped dancing. I turned around, still playing the fiddle, and saw that men had blocked all the windows, the doors. Mr. Samuel Stephens and Mr. Joseph Sellers from the Society for the Reformation of Manners led the constable's men in and asked us to produce Thomas Phillips known as Sally.

Eccleston said, "He ain't here."

They loaded us with chains and put us in carts and drove the men to Newgate and Margaret Clapp off to The Compter. Eccleston and Gabriel Lawrence held a loud conversation between themselves about how lying was okay but blowing up on your friends was not. "Not that anyone in the cart ever did anything," Eccleston said. They figured they'd had stuck their dicks in the wrong boys, but perhaps the informants didn't have information on all of us. "Save yourself, don't take anyone with you," Lawrence said.

Forty men. We didn't think we'd all hang, but we knew some would. Nobody got much sleep. In the morning, the troops got us together and put us in carts again and drove us to various Justices' of the Peace houses. We went in with the informants. I gave my name and said I was just the fiddler. A doctor pulled my pants down and checked for evidence, but I was clean. Stephens and Sellers hadn't heard anything about me since I'd come to play at Mother Clapp's after their visits. Partridge wasn't going anywhere near the people who'd been captured, just in case anyone would be willing to die to crack his eggs.

The Justice of the Peace said, "If you're a skilled fiddler, there are more respectable places that will have you play. You can go, just don't ever come before me again."

I bobbed my head. My kinswomen had heard at Newgate where I was being taken, and their fast cab got them to the Justice of the Peace's house just after the cart that brought us down from Newgate. They showed up as I was being released, but introduced themselves to the Justice of the Peace as my fiancé and her sister. I gave both an enthusiastic kiss, which seemed to cheer the Justice of the Peace and win me much butch het cred. After we paid my release fee, I went back with them to the shop and lathered myself in louse-killing shampoo, moved everything from my rented rooms into the shop, and did what I usually do, worked for my family.

Meanwhile, Thomas Newton went to bail Mother Clapp and was taken himself. Something broke him, probably fear of hanging since he'd slept with at least someone in at least three or four molly houses. He turned informant. April 13, a week before the trials, Eccleston died in Newgate Prison, in the company of his friends and a couple of mollies who hadn't been imprisoned who didn't give a damn about being known as his friends. I'm ashamed to say I wasn't one of them.

The old man was spared from the public misery of hanging. The Society for the Reformation of Morals scraped a vicious piece of work, Ned Courtney, out of some sewer and went after others using him for evidence. He was 18; three employers turned him out because he stole, threw temper tantrums, and tried blackmail on the side.

One man, George Kegar, was condemned on Courtney's evidence. Kegar had begged off fucking Ned because of an injury. Ned didn't take the no kindly and offered up his younger brother if Kegar didn't think he was handsome enough. Later, after Ned lost his last post, Kegar advised him to stop whoring and threatening blackmail, but that was all Ned knew how to do. Kegar wouldn't give Ned money; Ned claimed Kegar fucked him. The molly world thought Ned was testifying for money.

Another man, Courtney's last master, George Whittle, told the court that Ned had been in Newgate three times, that his first accuser had been the wife of a man who'd cheated him and who had herself been to Newgate for perjury. Then the only remaining witness, who'd testified that he'd seen men with their cocks out in a back room talking about one being the best and one being Battersea'ed, heard Whittle's testimony that what he witnessed was a clap clinic that young surgeon friends of Whittle's ran about eight times a week. A Battersea'ed cock was one in need of treatment, the ingredient coming from Battersea Market.

Yeah, whatever. Ned admitted to all his visits to Newgate, including the one involving a fight in a molly house, and claimed they were all someone else's fault or the liquor. Ned always lived in molly houses until people threw him out. The jury decided it would rather believe Whittle ran a venereal disease clinic than convict again on Ned's testimony.

Whittle was acquitted and Kegar reprieved. Both of them were better off than the average mollies. Kegar had been a schoolmate of Tom Orme's, who ran a molly house that employed Ned Courtney. Whittle owned property.

Thomas Wright ran his house in rented rooms. Much to everyone's horror, Wright, who hadn't a keen memory of the attacks on mollies in 1707 and no living children, blabbed to the prison ordinary, the chaplain who did sleaze

journalism on the side. The ordinary published his account
of what all the condemned men said. Gabriel Lawrence
and William Griffin, who'd lived at Mother Clapp's, still
refused to admit anything. Gabriel and William had children from earlier marriages. Lawrence's wife was dead.
Griffin's, I never heard much about.

Mother Clapp wasn't tried in April.

On May 5, Kegar was reprieved (someone finally noticed that his story was more reasonable than Ned's), and
the death sentences of the others confirmed. Before May
9, 1726, parties unknown buggered the Tyburn bleacher
seats, from which the rich watched the hangings up close.
Three carts went out from Newgate in a slow three-mile
procession to Tyburn, a traffic-jammed parade of the condemned. The first carried Lawrence, Wright, and Griffin;
the second carried three highwaymen; the third carried
two housebreakers and a murderer who'd helped a woman
kill her husband. The woman was dragged on a sledge to
be burned. Mounted soldiers surrounded all the carts and
the sledge.

I had gone ahead to Tyburn before the crowds following the carts arrived. Just before the execution, the
bleacher seats for the rich collapsed. A young molly I'd
never noticed before came up, dressed as a woman, but
she smelled like a boy. He stood with his back against my
belly. I put my hand on his shoulder, and he squeezed my
hand. Those of us who'd die today would have friends in
the crowd. When the first cart got to Tyburn, two dead
and several injured from the bleachers had been carried
off. I saw Gabriel Lawrence look at the damaged bleachers as his cart pulled up to Tyburn's hanging tree, a frame
of three beams across three posts, each post far enough
apart for a cart to pull in.

Centuries Ago and Very Fast

As the cart was pushed backward under the first beam, Gabriel figured out that the bleacher seats had collapsed, maybe guessed why or even knew why, and smiled. I found his eyes and held them. Someone friendly would be in the crowd. His eyes searched the crowd, stopped momentarily and then moved back to the two of us, then moved on again. We weren't the only friends in the crowd. I kept my hand on the young molly's shoulder. People had already climbed back into what was left of the bleachers. The nooses were already on the men's necks, the long end of the ropes wound around their waists, their hands were tied in front of them. They all had white caps on.

The hangman's assistants began unwinding the ropes and tossed the free ends up to their master on top of the beam. He tied each one off, taut, no drop. The ordinary prayed over the men. Lawrence and Griffin, both older men with children they didn't want hurt by this, looked annoyed when Wright confessed yet again. Lawrence looked back at someone in the crowd, someone closer to him than I'd been, and Griffin simply closed his eyes. The hangman gave the signal, his assistants pulled the caps down over the men's faces, and the cart man whipped the horses to pull the cart away, leaving the men choking in the ropes.

Two of the highwaymen took this opportunity to try escaping, throwing off their halters and ropes tying their hands. One got out of the cart before he was stopped. The other didn't make it out of the cart. They were hanged next, then the murderer and housebreakers on the third beam.

The two older men died first, then Wright. The highwaymen were still alive when the cart was driven out from under the last three. Wright finally died, and the anatomy students cut down Lawrence's body. The molly standing in front of me groaned.

The scaffolding began making creaking sounds in the silence of the crowd waiting for the last men to finally die and for Catherine Hayes to be burned. When the urine finally ran, the executioner got Hayes fastened to the stake. She was having fits over it, begging the executioner to strangle her first. He started the fire and botched the strangling job. The fire was too hot for him to keep pulling on the rope threaded around her neck and through the post she was tied to. She screamed and tried to kick away the burning faggots. Someone threw a chunk of wood at her head. That wasn't enough — another chunk and the eyes melted out of her head.

The scaffolding collapsed again, then again in another place.

The molly in front of me reached into his skirts and pulled out a bolt that had been cut halfway through. Without turning to face me, he showed me the bolt, quickly, and put it away again.

Six of them for four of us, and more to die of the injuries.

I squeezed his shoulder again hard. I don't know if Griffin's boy and girl got their father's body to bury, and hoped that nobody attacked them because of their father's conviction. He said that they'd turned out to be fine children. Lawrence also left a child, a 13-year-old daughter.

The molly slipped away in the crowd as we turned away from the ashes and the wrecked scaffolding. I hadn't gotten a good look at his face.

I walked back to my family's shop and sat down in the back garden and cried. Isobel and Rose found me there and led me back in the house and set up a big tin tub to wash in, and I soaked in louse-killing suds. They dried me off and fed me a sleeping draught of opium and put me to bed in fresh boiled sheets over a clean straw mattress.

"Don't stay for Mother Clapp's trial," Isobel said. "No good can come of it."

"Will you let me know if you hear from Sal?"

"We'll do that. We'll put something in the ledgers if we hear from him."

In the morning, I felt like I was abandoning friends, but I could see where I'd come from, and it was a matter of stepping over.

Whatever I'd done, it was done.

"What happens?" Isobel asked.

"Things change drastically, beginning with the steam engines and spinning machines. I should tell you that woolen mills in the north will be a great investment, and coal becomes even more useful with coking mills. And cotton becomes very big. But remember to leave me some Hogarths and put the stump work somewhere safe from mold. There will be a Jacobean rebellion in Scotland, but it will fail."

And then the railroad and telegraph beyond their lifetimes, and steam ships cutting the time between continents to days rather than weeks. The next 300 years would change more than the last 3000. I wondered if they'd be alive for the revolutionary end of this century, what they as old ladies would think of it. They'd be in their late nineties, but even the time-bound people in my family live long lives.

I came home and spent most of the next two weeks in my rooms, making the video of the queens with full skirts swarming out of the ancient house, soaring off into the skies.

Then went to Amsterdam where I bathed in hot wet boys, simple brainless safe sex, and spooge for another two weeks until I felt ridiculous.

In the pages of an old store account book, between November 28 and 29, 1726, was a draft against a merchant bank for what we were owed for the clothes. Isobel and Rose never bothered to cash it. Sal made it to the New World alive, sold the clothes for a profit, and paid us back. I wondered who got the money when we didn't cash in the draft, and turned the next page of the ledger and found a letter:

> *Met a friend on Ship. Hes a laydees taylor. We marryed wimen like your sisters. Herd ab't Clapp and all. Nasty blowing bitches.*
>
> *Philadelphia is smaller than Brighton, and twice as boring, but beats hanging.*
>
> *Thomas*

I wished them joy of each other, in whatever combinations of their quartet and the temporal equivalent of turkey-basters that worked for them.

Slash is for Girls

In the past, I've been encouraged, almost forcibly, to do children's books or young adult fiction. Women are supposed to be good at things for children and not so good at subversion or irony. But I didn't like children, and I'd never read YA as a high school student. I *had* written porn. So here is my slash that's not based on other people's characters—though I suspect Vel is kin to Charles Simic's long-lived character in "The Dancing Reindeer," and I've stuck in some other people from various places.

Slash is women's fiction not intended for children. It features characters from already existing fiction having sex with each other, for instance, Kirk/Spock, Jack Aubrey/Jack Sparrow. The slash is the connection/disconnection. The women who write slash fan fiction collaborate, share, and reappropriate stolen cultural archetypes and put them in bed with each other.

Some professional writers sneer at fan slash because it doesn't use original characters, while others are horrified that the fans are raping the characters they'd created. However, typical commercial fiction isn't known for using particularly original characters either—the vampires, the sea captains, the star ship captains, the doctor who is a good listener — so the fanfic writers are taking back the archetypes of our age and giving them erotic lives beyond what the original creator was willing to put to paper. Rowling didn't invent child wizards or boarding school novels any more than I invented time travelers. Fiction is all a pastiche, and slash is about the beds we get out of to put on our official roles.

The net gave women a way to share slash fanfic while reducing the chance of annoying the people who'd copyrighted their themes and variations on the archetypical people of our time — the technical boys, the fighting space or sea warriors.

My first introduction to fanfic was the Star Wars community, but I wasn't paying much attention then. Finally, Kirrily Roberts, known as Skud, and her friends working with Hornblower/Jack Aubrey/Pirates of the Caribbean fanfic and vids forced me to pay attention. Skud's "Shore Leave" was a big fuck puddle of characters from all those sources.

The quality varied. One of the Harry Potter slash stories in the Live Journal community, Pornish Pixies, set in New Orleans, was quite good; a story that had been posted the day before was not so good. Pornish Pixies had to fight the Live Journal management to keep from being eliminated in the big Live Journal/Six Apart porn crackdown — the management of LJ didn't want to imagine that imaginary children (adolescents) could be imagined (drawn) as having sex.

Slash is what women do when they're entertaining themselves. It's brutally realistic about teenagers and their desires for each other and the likelihood that teen sex will happen despite laws prohibiting sex for the sexually mature but underaged. In slash, men are the emotional ones, which is nothing new in gay women's writing (see Mary Renault). Many of the slash writers are gay or bisexual women. The men become the women become the men. Slash explores what the most other of the opposite sex might be doing in bed and feeling about it. And gay men are like women in that society's primary definition of them is sexual first.

And women, straight or gay, appear to be aroused by any known combination of sexes.

By stealing other people's characters, the women who write slash are either re-appropriating characters from the common stock or being conservative in their imaginations along one axis while filling the voids in the canonical material.

I look at it as pastiche; as a collective dance through the sexual ids; as not thinking about motherhood and writing for children; as writing for people who are adult women.

The hostile way to look at it is as a failure of nerve, a failure to invent the characters as well as how the characters have sex. Or sneaking into other people's gardens to play with their garden gnomes. The critic who says that the slash writers are failing to learn how to invent credible characters is not considering how all fictional characters are made up of words and originally came from other writers' words or are drawn from life. (We can more easily confess to stealing other people's characters than to basing our characters on real people.)

So Vel showed up with a guitar and a skill with computer graphics; the character who is Thomas evolved out of memories of one man in SF who'd been a cop in some place like Iowa before moving to SF to be a moderately out gay guy, of a gay housemate who'd been an interrogator in Vietnam, and of some other people and some other fictional characters. Other characters in these stories populated a novel version, but what I found I cared about were the stories Vel told his lovers, and the stories his lovers had to tell.

The challenge for me was to make the sex scenes both pornish (as in makes you hot) and definitive of the characters. How we are in bed and what we imagine other people are doing in bed defines who we are as people as much as any other part of our lives does.

Vel can tell stories for almost forever.